A NOVEL

THE STREAM

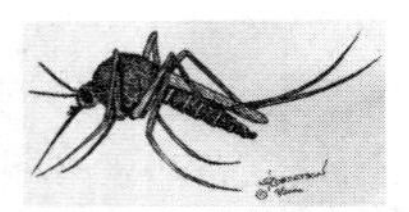

PUBLISHED BY HIGH PITCHED HUM PUBLISHING
321 15th Street North
Jacksonville Beach, Florida 32250
www.jettyman.com
www.ranchboybooks.com

HIGH PITCHED HUM and the mosquito are trademarks
of High Pitched Hum Publishing

All of the events in this book are fictitious, and any resemblance
to actual persons, living or dead, is purely coincidental.

The cataloging-in-publication data is on file with the Library
of Congress

ISBN 0-9777290-7-9

Contact H. Steven Robertson at coachrtoo@yahoo.com.
Neptune Beach, Florida

Printed in the United States of America

July 2006

THE STREAM

A NOVEL

H. STEVEN ROBERTSON

HIGH PITCHED HUM PUBLISHING
Jacksonville Beach, Florida USA

BOOKS BY H. STEVEN ROBERTSON

RANCH BOY - a novel featuring Robbie Duncan

ACORNS OF LOVE AND WISDOM - poetry

SOCCER MADE EASY FOR AMERICANS - how to book

BOTTOM TIME, a novel also featuring Robbie Duncan

THE STREAM – a novel

AN EXERCISE MANUAL FOR THE COUCH POTATO – a joke book

Coming soon: UNTIL DEATH DO US PART – a novel

GOOD 'OLE BOY, DOWN HOME RECIPES – a cookbook

SPECIAL THANKS

Special thanks go to Dr. Dana Thomas for her excellent editing comments and for taking time to do it. They go also to Vanessa Wells and Anne Berkey for their help and to G. W. Reynolds III (Billy) for his undying support and assistance. We are all having so much fun.

And I can't begin the express the gratitude due my wife Kathy for putting up with a guy who spends countless hours on the computer while she takes up the slack around the house. Also, special thanks for her excellent editing comments.

PROLOGUE

Sandy knew he was in serious trouble when he looked up and saw the billowing blue-black clouds with the brilliant sabers of lightning stabbing downward, rolling toward him over darkening seas. His nineteen-foot powerless boat lay dead in the water twenty-five miles from shore in the Atlantic Ocean. At fourteen years old, Sandy was the archetypical middle school aged boy. He was small because his growth spurt hadn't kicked in yet, and he was 5'6" tall. He kept his sandy blond hair cropped close, and his age caused a few ugly pimples to form on his face. Sandy was a loner. He had a few friends and mostly he kept to himself. He was also a boy of few words just like his father and a lot of the other fishermen who lived in Mayport, Florida. This caused most of the students at Mayport Middle School to misunderstand him and think he was arrogant and egotistical. The only time Sandy talked a lot was when it was about his beloved nature or fishing.

Although Sandy was thin, he was very wiry and strong, but that didn't show in his outward appearance. Fishermen's sons had hands like rocks, made so by hauling in ropes and lines and performing the labor-intensive work on a fishing boat. Sandy had high cheekbones and bright blue eyes. His eyes had the look of a person who spent a lot of time out of doors, either on the sea or in wide-open spaces. He had the same piercing look in his eyes that could be seen in a hawk or an eagle.

The gusts of cold wind that always preceded a storm began to blow against Sandy and the boat. It was being pushed further and further from shore.

It was two-thirty in the afternoon. For the first time, Sandy started to feel fear. He realized he had been foolish. Thoughts were coursing through his head.

I've been cocky and stupid! I know better. You don't mess around with the ocean because she'll get cha' if you screw up. I should have told my dad where I was going. The only person who knows is Mr. Johnny, and he won't know I haven't come back. Johnny thinks I was going to Nine Mile. I just had to get greedy and try to get that one more fish when I had plenty. I had to forget that a huge storm was on the way. My boat is ruined, the engine is dead, the radio is dead, the battery is burned up and that monster storm is coming. I must be over twenty-five or thirty miles from shore, and the storm is pushing me further out. If I don't start using my head, I'll die out here.

Sandy took a piece of line and tied the fishing poles up under the port gunwale. He pulled the massive cobia he caught over and slid it under the tarp with the four kingfish. It was almost as large as he was. All he could do was shake his head. It was the best day fishing he'd ever had in his life, and it was probably all for nothing. He took another piece of line and looped it through a grommet on the canvas that covered the fish and tied it to the stern cleat. He had three one-gallon jugs of water left, and he tied those down as well.

He knew he was in for a blow; the seas had already picked up. The boat was tossing pretty heavily now. The storm would wash anything not tied down overboard, and Sandy knew he would need all of the things he had for what he could face in the future, which was frighteningly uncertain now. The cooler and tackle box were tied off also. The wind was blowing angry seas out of the west, and the boat turned sideways to them, which threatened to capsize it.

Sandy tied his sea anchor to the bow and threw it in. This acted like a parachute and kept the boat pointed in the direction of the sea so the bow, as it was designed to do, split the waters as if it was in motion. He was also careful to don a life preserver and tie a rope around his waist. He would die if he was washed overboard and lost contact with the boat.

The small boat with the young boy and five giant fish was being pushed farther and farther from shore. Sandy was already over thirty miles from the docks in Mayport. The wind was howling around him now like a whole posse of banshees on horseback. The waves grew higher and higher, undulating like cars on a roller coaster. They crashed over the gunwales of his little nineteen-foot fishing boat. Then the rain began. It blew down sideways in choking sheets that stung his face and filled his nostrils when he looked into it. He was glad for the rain slicker he always kept on the boat, because that gave him some protection. Regardless how hard

Sandy bailed with the white, five-gallon bucket; the boat was slowly filling with water.

With his outboard engine knocked out and his radio down, the youngster was at the mercy of the elements. The world was getting darker and darker. The waves had kicked up to almost ten feet. Only the sea anchor was saving him from being swamped. The boat raced further and further from shore as it was propelled by the treacherous western winds of the furious gale. Winds were blowing in gusts up to fifty miles per hour—almost hurricane strength. A sobering thought suddenly coursed through Sandy's mind. *Oh no. The Stream!* He was being pushed east toward the northeasterly flowing Gulf Stream.

The Gulf Stream was a warm surface current which originated in the Gulf of Mexico near the equator and flowed northeast across the Atlantic, driven by prevailing southwest winds. It influenced the climate of the United Kingdom and Northwest Europe by bringing with it warm, humid, and mild air. The ocean current traveled past the east coast of the United States towards Newfoundland. The North Atlantic Drift formed an extension to the Gulf Stream, which flowed past the south coast of Labrador toward the west coast of Europe. The water in the stream was very warm, having been heated in the relatively shallow areas of the Gulf of Mexico. The water traveled at speeds that varied between one and three miles per hour.

Sandy was a small boy in a huge, furious, and unforgiving ocean. His frightened mind could only focus on a series of events over the past two weeks that led up to this perilous predicament.

CHAPTER I – TURN ABOUT IS FAIR PLAY

"Hey, guys, look at the panty waist with the bald head. Hey, sissy, I'll bet you like the guys, huh? Hey, butt head, I'm talking to you!" Bart Jenkins was an eighth grader and the bully of Mayport Middle School. Typical of bullies, he preyed on the smaller boys and showed off for the other students while doing it. Bart was one of the students who physically matured way ahead of the others. Of course, the fact that he had repeated the third and seventh grades made him much older too. At sixteen years of age, Bart was just an inch shy of six feet tall. He had long dirty black hair, a big Roman-like nose, and ebony eyes. He was also pudgy and soft, a fact he chose to ignore. Today, Sandy Stevens, a seventh grader, was his target.

Sandy tried to ignore Bart's obnoxious comments and the other students who were laughing at him. This only served to encourage the bully more. Unfortunately, Sandy was very unpopular with the students who didn't understand his quiet and shy nature. They loved to see Sandy ridiculed, and they pointed and hooted as Bart continued.

"See, you guys, he is a sissy. He won't even stop and defend himself. Hey, pimple face, why don't you go cry to your mommy? I'm sure she'll wipe your tears and call you a good little boy."

The other students roared with laughter, and Sandy stopped and turned to face this taunting bully. He was furious and ashamed. His mind was ablaze with thoughts. *One day, I'll teach that slimy fat pig a lesson. I don't like to fight, but I'm not afraid of him. It's just not worth getting suspended for. One punch in that big pot gut and follow it with a right to the chin. We'll see who cries to his mother then.*

Bart was enjoying the attention he was getting at Sandy's expense, and the crowd loved it. "Well, lookey here. This puny little sissy's askin' for a butt whippin'. Come on, sissy, do something." Bart drew himself up to his almost six-feet height and sneered a slimy green-toothed smile down at Sandy. His dental hygiene wasn't any better than his weight control.

The grin, however, was short lived. To be called a *sissy* in front of the other students was too much. What Bart didn't realize was that Sandy had an older brother. Even though they loved each other, the boys often fought. Their father had taught them to box at an early age. He believed in his boys' ability to take care of themselves. Since his older brother was much bigger and more powerful, the end result was Sandy became a significantly better fighter. Plus, Mayport Village was a rough place. The boys who lived there had to know how to defend themselves, and fights were quite common.

The big bully was sure he had the smaller Sandy where he wanted him. He was excited about showing the other students what a big man he was and he was reveling from their enjoyment as taunted the unpopular youngster.

Suddenly, Sandy exploded. He dropped his books, and his foot shot up and connected with Bart directly between his legs. The wind came out of Bart like exhaust from a school bus. He grabbed himself and bent over in pain. As his face came down, Sandy's rock-hard fist rose up, and he rammed it into Bart's nose. With that, the confrontation was over. Bart groveled on the ground with one hand holding his nose and the other holding between his legs. He slobbered and bawled like a baby as he writhed about.

The other students had gotten very quiet. Sandy turned slowly, looking each one of them in the eye. They hadn't been prepared for what they just witnessed. Sandy bent over, picked up his books, and walked toward his next class. He knew he would be getting a call from the principal's office soon, but he didn't care. One thing was for certain. News traveled fast, and nobody would taunt Sandy again.

Few students understood Sandy. His shy nature was misinterpreted for arrogance, and he didn't make many friends. None of them knew the real reason, however, and it was because Sandy's real love in life was the outdoors. He loved being on the water more than anything and felt a true kinship with the creatures that lived there. In addition, his father was a commercial fisherman. All fishermen respected toughness in their sons, and even though Sandy would probably be suspended for the fight, his father would be proud of him. The other thing was his dad bought him a boat that he could take out by himself whenever he wished. It was a nineteen-foot fiberglass deep "V" hulled craft with a 100 horsepower Evinrude engine. The engine was mounted on the transom in the stern of the boat. A steering console was bolted forward in the center of the deck. The boat was a little older, but it was in excellent shape and was painted white. The engine was used but in very good condition. One thing that was common about all commercial fishermen's boats was the boat was usually older, but the engines were almost always relatively new.

Sandy lived to be out in his boat. Whether he was on the waterway or on the St. Johns River or on the Atlantic Ocean, he was home. His father had taken him on many fishing trips since he was a little boy. He saw and experienced things few boys his age had, and he became an excellent boatman. Sandy's father put no restraints on his use of the boat. As long as his grades were up in school and he acted like a man, Sandy could go where he pleased. Sandy also realized that if he were suspended, it would give him that many more days to run about in his boat.

"Miss Wells!" The squawk box that served as a public address speaker on the wall sprung to life in Sandy's classroom. All the students looked at Sandy whose face remained blank. Knowing what was coming next, Sandy started gathering his things. "Please send Sandy Stevens to Mr. Reynolds' office." Miss Wells was Sandy's favorite teacher. She was young, brunette, and very pretty. She looked over at Sandy.

"Sandy, I guess you're wanted in Mr. Reynolds' office. You better take your books; it isn't long until the bell rings." Sandy stood up without saying a word, picked up his books, and headed for the door. *Ain't it great; I'm goin' fishin'.* He walked proudly down the hall toward the principal's office.

Sandy stepped in through the open door to Mr. Reynolds' outer office. The secretary was expecting him. "Hi, Sandy. Go right on in. Mr. Reynolds is waiting for you."

Bart was sitting in a chair facing Mr. Reynolds' desk. His nose was swollen and bright red. Both eyes had started to blacken, and his cheeks were tear-stained. Bart was a pitiful sight.

Mr. Reynolds was also the son of a fisherman. Having been raised in the little fishing village of Mayport, he understood the tough young men who grew up around the rigors of commercial fishing. He had to defend himself many times in his youth, and he was a tough, skillful fighter. Mr. Reynolds couldn't help but notice the tremendous difference in size between the two youths. Inwardly, he was proud of Sandy, but he couldn't let violent behavior be condoned in the school regardless of the reason.

"Have a seat, Sandy. Set your books on the corner of my desk. So what do you have to say for yourself? We've got a pretty beaten up fella' sitting here." Bart whimpered, which was disgusting to the veteran principal but he didn't let the feeling register on his face.

Sandy looked Mr. Reynolds straight in the eyes and didn't flinch. "He shouldn't a called me a *sissy*. He said he was gonna beat me up and called me pimple face. I had to take up for myself. That's the way I was taught by my dad."

Mr. Reynolds understood about how Mayport fishermen raised their sons. He turned his attention back to Bart. "You say bad things about Sandy, Bart?"

Bart started crying again. He was blubbering as he talked. "I didn't mean anything. I was just kiddin' him. He kicked me in my privates when I wasn't expecting it. I didn't touch him first. Look what he done to my face."

Mr. Reynolds knew this could be a touchy situation. He had met with Bart's parents before and realized that they were the major reason this boy was so messed up. No matter what the truth was, they would defend their derelict son's side of the story. They were belligerent and combative. No matter what his decision was, they would call and complain to his boss.

"Even if you didn't touch him, you had no reason to say awful things about him like that. Sandy, you didn't have a right to kick him or hit him either. There are better ways to work things out in a civilized society. I respect your right to defend yourself, but in this case no one has touched you."

"Mr. Reynolds, look at the size of this guy. If I let him get to me first, I wouldn't stand much of a chance. He may not have hit me first, but he was going to." Sandy was honest, spoke in a matter of fact voice, and looked Mr. Reynolds directly in the eyes when he talked. Mr. Reynolds loved it. But there was no way he could let on how much he respected this honest and tough little fellow even though he knew he was right.

"Sandy, I understand what you are saying. Regardless, we can't have a school full of students who act like gunslingers and start fighting every time they don't like what is said to them." Mr. Reynolds suspected his punishment wouldn't hurt Sandy, because he knew the boy would just go fishing. He had too, once upon a time. "Sandy, you stay home for the next three days on suspension. And Bart, you're just as guilty. You have a reputation of bullying, but it caught up to you this time. I suggest that you change your ways. You have three days home, too."

Bart started his disgusting sobbing again. Mr. Reynolds handed him a tissue. "Both of you go to the outer office and get your parents on the phone. Tell them you have been suspended and ask them to come pick you up."

Sandy stood up and offered his hand to Mr. Reynolds. "Yes sir, Mr. Reynolds. I'm sorry I let you down." He shook Mr. Reynolds' hand, picked up his books, and walked to the outer office.

Sandy's father pulled up in front of the school in his dusty, black Ford F-150 pickup truck with giant knobby tires. Steve Stevens looked like an older version of his son. He wasn't a large man, but his arms were wiry and strong from handling the ropes, fishing lines, and gear. He was a quiet man and rarely had much to say. This came from years of working alone on the sea. When he did speak, it was thought through, and his words were to the point. He walked into the principal's office and spotted Sandy sitting in a chair. Steve motioned to Sandy and walked over to the secretary's desk. "Mornin'. I'm Sandy's dad. I'd like to see Mr. Reynolds."

He was ushered into Mr. Reynolds office, and the two men shook hands. "Hi, Bill. Can you tell me what my youngin's done now?" The two men had known each other their entire lives, although they weren't close friends.

"No problem. Sandy, wait in the outer office for a minute, and close the door when you leave." After Sandy had closed the door, Mr. Reynolds turned back to Steve, relaxed and chuckled. "To put it simple, Steve, Sandy kicked this big bully's butt. I'm pretty sure the boy has a broken nose."

"Sandy start the fight?"

"Not really. The other kid has a reputation for picking on smaller kids. He shows off for the other students by doing it. He called Sandy *Pimple Face* and *Sissy* and then bowed up at him like he was going to fight. Sandy kicked him between his legs and punched him in the nose. It was over before it started. You know I understand and don't blame Sandy. I respect his guts. He is also a gentleman. You have raised him well. I'm in a bind, however. I have a fight taking place in the halls and a boy who's pretty beaten up. I have to set an example. But, three days won't hurt Sandy."

Steve extended his hand once more to Mr. Reynolds. "I understand. Good seein' ya' again, Bill." With that, he turned and walked out of the office. He put his hand on Sandy's shoulder as they quietly walked back to the truck.

The big Ford engine roared to life. "Ya' had to hit him, didn't cha' boy?"

"Yessir, he woulda' hit me first if I didn't do something. I got tired of him pickin' on me so I blasted him where it hurt."

Steve didn't say anything for a while as the truck headed back to the fishing village. "I don't blame ya' none. Man's gotta' do what he's gotta' do." That's all that was said the entire trip back to Mayport.

CHAPTER II – THE PENALTY

Sandy threw his books on the bed in his room and changed into a tee shirt and shorts. It was only a short walk from his home on Palmer Street to Matt Roland's docks. Sandy's dad sold his catch to Matt and was allowed dock space because of it. This particular dock was where Cap'n Bill Aley docked his snapper boat, the *Restless*.

Sandy called his boat *Out Back*. He had heard the name at the movies when he saw *Crocodile Dundee*. Not only did he love that movie, the name and the scenery in the movie reminded him of his favorite places which were up the river and up and down the Intracoastal Waterway. Because of laws that protected the estuarial system and the tidal flats from growth and development, most of it was wild and pristine.

The Intracoastal Waterway was 3,000 miles long, providing sheltered passage for commercial and leisure boats along the U.S. Atlantic coast from Boston, Massachusetts, to Key West, Florida. It also ran along the Gulf of Mexico coast from Apalachee Bay, Florida, to Brownsville, Texas. It was partly natural and partly man made. The Intracoastal Waterway also had a good deal of commercial activity; barges hauled petroleum, petroleum products, foodstuffs, building materials, and manufactured goods.

Out Back was moored to the dock and was bobbing gently up and down in the current. Sandy took off his white fisherman's boots and threw them into the boat, lowered a couple of fishing poles and a tackle box down, then leapt spryly onto the floor. He reached back up on the dock and lowered the large cooler with ice, some drinks, and a couple of sandwiches down. Sandy walked to the stern and pulled up a baited trap he had tied off on the dock there. It was loaded with mud minnows he would use for bait. He poured these into a bucket of water that sat next to the starboard gunwale and lowered the trap back into the water.

Sandy turned the key, and the Evinrude came to life amid a puff of blue smoke. Outboards were relatively nasty engines as far as the environment was concerned. He let the engine warm up at idle while he pulled off his shirt and untied the ropes from the dock. The young man was in his natural element, and he was enthralled by it. He loved the boats. He loved the docks and slips. He loved the rustic and dilapidated old buildings that lined the banks of the river. Sandy grinned at a thought that suddenly ran through his head. *Some punishment, huh! I get to beat the punk's butt and go fishing because of it. Ain't life grand?*

The tide was coming in, and the water in the St. Johns River was flowing swiftly up river toward Jacksonville. *Out Back* was moored so that the bow was facing the flow of the water. The river at this point had turned north. One of the huge car-carrying ships loomed like a giant horizontal skyscraper on the river as it rumbled past Sandy. He pushed the throttle in gear and eased away from the dock, still heading toward the flow of the water. The current going past the boat caused it to appear stationary relative to the bank as

Sandy eased *Out Back* toward the opening in the docks that led to the channel.

One thing Sandy did religiously was to overstock his boat with drinking water. He always had at least four gallons in the box with the life jackets under the seat behind the steering console. He had read that a person could exist a long time without food, but their days would be numbered to about four without drinking water. Sandy was an avid reader and devoured adventure stories. He especially liked Hemingway. He fancied himself as one of these adventurers, and one never knew when he could get stuck somewhere like the *Ancient Mariner* with a lot of salt water around him but no fresh water to drink. *Water, water everywhere and nary a drop to drink.* Sandy loved that line from Samuel Taylor Coleridge from the poem they had read in English Class.

Sandy pulled a sandwich and a cola from the cooler and ate with one hand while steering with the other. The mustard and mayonnaise tasted great on the ham and cheese sandwich. He was headed up river for the waterway. It was just after twelve noon, and he had the whole afternoon to himself.

All events of the morning had left Sandy's head. When he ventured outdoors, he became at one with all of nature. The beautiful April day was clear and calm. On the river, the air had a wonderful, clean smell to it. The sun was directly overhead, and there was only a slight chop on the water.

A pod of young dolphins rolled beside him as he cruised past. No matter how many times he saw dolphins, he never tired of watching them. Actually, he considered naming his boat *The Dolphin* and almost did before he saw the movie and was captured by the adventurous name. Actually, Sandy never tired of watching any living thing whether it was plant or animal. Seagulls and brown pelicans were sitting on the shrimp boats, piers and docks and spiraling rapidly around above them. He was amused by a giant blue heron that was flying almost the exact speed and in the same direction as the boat. It slowly flapped its long graceful wings and flew along right beside him. Watching the huge wings made him think of the Wright Brothers and how they studied seagulls in flight when designing wings for their first airplane.

Sandy had finished his sandwich and was chomping on an apple when he pulled alongside the giant car carrier that was still steaming up river. A man walked out of the side door of the bridge and waved down to him. It was Cap'n Eric Bryson, one of the St. Johns River Bar Pilots. There weren't many places to eat in Mayport, and almost all the locals knew each other from the association. When he grew up, Sandy wanted a job like Eric had—one that kept him on the river and sea his whole life.

When *Out Back* got to the end of the Little Jetties south of Mayport, Sandy dropped the engine to idle speed. The mouth of the waterway here was a restricted area. The much-adored creatures called manatees cruised this area frequently. Boat propellers took a deadly toll on the species resulting in restricted speed zones in many parts of the river and waterway. Not complying would result in a heavy fine.

The tide was now flowing from behind him, and it was pushing his boat at a nice pace even though he was idling. He sped up again as he passed the sign signifying the end of the no wake zone. Now acres of undulating grassy tidal flats extended on both sides of the waterway. Tributaries and rivulets crisscrossed the plains of grass. Fish would be following the tide in to gorge themselves on creatures exposed by the onrushing water. The beautiful tidal flats with its undulating waves of emerald green sea grass were exactly where Sandy wanted to be.

CHAPTER III – THE KING OF BULLIES

The ride home had gone quite differently for Bart. Obadiah Jenkins professed to be fundamentalist Christian, but, he was a hypocrite. He didn't practice what he preached. Obadiah was built like Boss Tweed. He was tall and stout, looking for all the world like a huge watermelon with skinny arms and legs. He kept his hair trimmed in a flattop, hoping it would fool people into thinking he was a big, former athlete.

Obadiah's job as a used car salesman kept the family in plenty of money, and the poor suckers who bought his junk left with mechanical problems. He had the same nose his son used to have before Sandy rearranged it. Obadiah Jenkins was also swollen with false pride. With an ego as large as his protruding belly, he barged through life, bullying anyone who didn't fight back. His son was following in his father's footsteps like a true chip off the ol' block.

Mr. Reynolds had to use every bit of self-restraint he possessed to keep his composure when Obadiah stormed into his office unannounced. Obadiah towered above Mr. Reynolds.

"What the hell kind of school are you running here, Reynolds? Look at my son! He has a broken nose and who knows what else. You'll be hearing from my lawyers tomorrow! How could you let a big bully do this to my son? You will *not* suspend my son."

They always did that. People like Obadiah were really cowards at heart and always tried to use scare tactics and threats. How many times in his career had Mr. Reynolds heard the *lawyer* threat?

Mr. Reynolds was not intimidated. He spoke very calmly and quietly. "Mr. Jenkins, first of all, you can calm down and quit cussing, or you can leave my office. Second, your son was calling the other boy names and threatening him. The other boy is much younger and half the size of your son. It was not a *big* bully."

Obadiah's head snapped around to his pathetic looking son. "That boy was half your size? And you let him do this to you." He turned back to Mr. Reynolds. "What did you give the other boy?"

"He was suspended three days for fighting also."

"Bart didn't start the fight. I demand that you remove the suspension."

"Taunting another student and bullying will not be tolerated. This is not the first time for Bart. The suspension stands."

Obadiah's face flushed red when he couldn't get his way, and his attempts to intimidate Bill Reynolds weren't working. "Come on, Bart. Let's get the hell outta here." He spun Bart around and shoved him toward the door. "You'll be hearing from me, Reynolds. I'll have your job. I've got connections, you know. I pay your salary! You are done. Everyone in the neighborhood talks about how incompetent you are. It is time somebody does something about it, and I'm just the man to do it."

How many times in his career had Mr. Reynolds heard the, "I'll-have-your-job", line? It was another threat incompetent parents often used. And the clincher was, "I pay your salary!" Just because education was funded by tax dollars, weaklings like this would try to twist it as if they were paying educators' salaries.

Muttering under his breath, the Watermelon-on-legs rumbled out of the office and slammed the door as he left. Ironically, the School Resource Officer, Clarence Jerrell, was standing in the outer office talking to Mr. Reynolds' secretary. He was assigned to the school by the sheriff. He had seen the furious man enter the school and knew of his bullying tactics, so he hurried to the outer office in case he was needed. Officer Jerrell was standing outside the door listening, making sure the irate father didn't overstep his bounds.

"Stop right where you are, Mr. Jenkins."

Obadiah Jenkins, true to form for bullies, weakened quickly when it came to a force greater than his. His face flushed again, but this time it was from embarrassment at being caught throwing his tantrum. Officer Jerrell, opened the door to the outer office. "Come with me to my office, Mr. Jenkins. We need to have a talk."

Obadiah was stammering now. "Wha, ah, er, I'm sorry. I just got a little heated, that's all. Look at my boy's face. I'm really in a hurry."

Officer Jerrell spoke quietly. "Mr. Jenkins, I hope you aren't in too big a hurry to ignore what I am asking you to do. Now, I'll ask you one more time. Please accompany me to my office."

Obadiah and Bart followed Officer Jerrell around the corner and into his office. Officer Jerrell closed the door and spoke calmly. "Mr. Jenkins, Bart, please have a seat." He walked around behind his desk and sat down in his swiveling chair.

The two did as Officer Jerrell requested and sat quietly waiting for what he said next. "Mr. Jenkins, you are not allowed to come to this school and display such a violent, threatening temper. Mr. Jenkins, you are not allowed to cuss and slam doors. Now this is the last time I'm warning you. There are laws that protect school personnel from the behavior you have just displayed, and I assure you, I will enforce the law even if it means taking you to jail." Officer Jerrell was still speaking softly. "Do I make myself clear, Mr. Jenkins?"

Obadiah's pride had been severely damaged. He was forced to give in with his son watching. His ego was too destroyed for words. He just nodded meekly and got up and walked out of the office. Bart followed timidly behind. Father and son looked like Tweedle Dee and Tweedle Dum as they bobbled out of the building. When they closed the doors of the posh Cadillac, the big bully turned on his son. Now here was somebody he could intimidate. He got a twisted pleasure out of seeing the big boy cower before him.

"I oughta hit you in your damn nose again. Whadda ya mean you let a little boy do this to you. If my friends find out I've got a coward for a son, I'll never hear the last of it." He started the car and put it in gear. Still smarting from the encounter with the police officer, however, he was careful to drive properly. He was sure he would be watched until he left the campus. "You make this right, you hear me? You better make this right. Do you understand me, Bart? Do I make myself clear to you?"

Bart was hanging his head in shame. He was also in quite a bit of pain. "Yes, Pa. You make yourself clear."

"Now I gotta get you to the damn doctor and get your nose looked at." Obadiah fell into silence with a head full of thoughts. He needed revenge. He had been shamed in front of his son. His son had been shamed in front of the whole school, which reflected on him. He had to get this cocky Reynolds fellow. "You make this right, Bart, I mean it!" Bart thought he knew just how to do get revenge, and he wouldn't be alone this time.

CHAPTER IV – OUT BACK

Fishing the estuarial system of the waterway was a special art. Many fishermen spent hours and days on end and rarely caught a thing, even though fish flourished nearby. The species sought, the bait used for each specific species, the tide, the moon phase, time of year, water temperature, how the bait presented, where you fished; all of these factors and more determined how successful the fisherman was. Sandy had grown up on the water. He didn't even think about what to do as he instinctively made the correct choices.

Another thing good fishermen did was network with each other. Knowledge about what was biting where and other details were vital to success. The tight-knit groups closely guarded their secrets and shared them with only their inner circle of mates. They felt that too many boats and too many fishermen existed these days for the limited number of fish available. Sandy's buddies let him in on information that red bass and flounder were running in the estuaries.

Sandy spotted the channel he was looking for on the east side of the waterway and guided *Out Back* towards the opening through the grass. The wide beam of the boat gave it a very shallow draft, which was perfect for getting way back in the tidal flats where the best fish were. He idled very slowly up the channel that snaked back and forth. He knew to stay wide on each turn where the water would be deeper. Silt tended to build up on the insides of the curves, and the moving tides washed the solid material from the outsides.

The beauty of the salt flats was astounding. Snowy egrets reflected in the still waters as they stood rigidly at attention, fishing for the little minnows that swam past, then plunged their spear sharp beaks into the water and emerged with one flipping from it. Red-winged black birds flew back and forth, landing occasionally on the grass and bushes that grew there. Their cheerful *tweedle deeee, tweedle deeee* echoed over the marsh. A black snake-necked anhinga suddenly popped its head above water with a flipping minnow in its beak from where it had been swimming below on one of its constant fishing sorties. The bowl shaped cloudless sky graced the scene with a beautiful, light blue canopy. To Sandy, this was his type of heaven.

He reached the part of the estuary where it had gotten almost too shallow for his boat to navigate and cut off the engine. There was a nice bend in the channel just ahead, and he knew fish liked to lurk on the inside of it where the silt had built up. He picked up his casting rod and hooked a mud minnow up through the mouth and flipped it out into the water. Slowly he reeled the bait back towards him. Nothing. He reeled it all the way in again and flipped it out a couple yards away from his first cast and started working the bait again. The water exploded, and his rod bent double.

"Gotcha! Ha!" He had a nice fish and from the pull on the line, he suspected it was a big red bass. Sandy kept the tip of his rod held high, so the pole could help fight the fish. He worked it back and forth, following the fish's direction in the water. When he pulled the fish up to the boat, he used his net to lift it out of the water. It was a red bass. Sandy had a yardstick screwed to the gunwale of his boat, and he held the beautiful fish up to it. Sixteen inches—too small to keep. Sandy had to release the fish, so he lay it gently in the water and let go. He hooked a new mud minnow and threw it out once again.

This time he got an enormous hit. The water erupted in a huge splash and the line was being stripped from his reel. He'd get a little line in, then the fish would strip it back off; a little more line in and then the drag would give, and the line would come back off. That was okay, because Sandy had intentionally set the drag so the fish couldn't stretch the line tight enough to break it.

Finally, the big fish started to tire out. He pulled a good-sized red to the side of the boat and used his net to get it out of the water. He held this one up to the yardstick. Twenty-six inches—just one inch within the legal limit. Reds that were kept by fishermen had to be between seventeen and twenty-seven inches in length. The red bass was a beautiful creature. It was covered with very large iridescent scales that were a pinkish brown in color. It had a huge head that dwarfed the rest of the body. Large, brown circular spots dotted its body randomly. Sandy liked reds because one of his favorite things to eat was blackened redfish. No other fish tasted as good blackened. They also brought a good price at the fish house. He opened the lid to the cooler and dropped it in. It was good that this fish was a big one, because the Florida Marine Patrol limited each fisherman to one redfish a day. They had been almost fished to extinction due to the blackened redfish fad that grew out of Louisiana thanks to Chef Prodhumme.

Now that he had a nice red in the cooler, Sandy was hoping to hook up on some flounder, so he started the outboard and eased back down the channel to the waterway. As he idled back out, his keen eyes searched the surface of the water around him. Then he spotted what he was looking for just ahead. He pulled the throttle into neutral and slipped his hand into the loop of line that was attached to his cast net. Finger mullet were superb flounder bait. These young fish swam in schools near the surface of the water, making V-shaped ripples in the water as they moved. He stood perfectly still so that the mullet would swim past him, and then he tossed the net over them.

Sandy no longer had a need for the mud minnows so he poured them out, refreshed the water and emptied the net full of finger mullet into the bucket. He got all the bait he needed in one cast. The little mullet were jumping out of the bucket, so Sandy threw his tee shirt over the top. He would need to refresh the water in the bucket often so the fish wouldn't asphyxiate themselves by depleting the oxygen in the water and replacing it with their metabolic wastes.

He knew a place near the ferry slip on the far side of river that always held good flounder. The water was relatively shallow, and the bottom was flat, just like flounder were fond of. Sandy was in the river once again, and directly across from Monty's Marina. A picturesque shrimp boat, black diesel exhaust trailing from the stack behind it, was chugging back to port from a shrimping expedition. Both booms were lowered to keep the craft from rocking as much when it traveled. When booms were up, so much weight overhead caused the boat to rock quite a bit. A horde of pirouetting seagulls and brown pelicans blanketed the sky above it, awaiting the free meal of trash fish the shrimpers would shovel overboard.

As *Out Back* got near the ferry slip, Sandy heard the captain announce over the PA system that the drivers should be warned of the loud ship's whistle, which went off just after the warning. He heard the giant diesel engines revving up as the huge *John Ribault* shuddered out of the slip and into the St. Johns River. As the big craft pulled out, it swung into the current and headed across the river to the ferry slip on the other bank.

Sandy tossed the anchor overboard and put a finger mullet on the hook. He had tied on a smaller hook this time. Sandy hooked a finger mullet up through its mouth and tossed the line out over the starboard gunwale and slowly reeled the bait back to the boat. The next cast would be slightly east of the first cast, and each succeeding toss of the line would gradually go to the side of the one before. He was trying to drag his bait in front of one of the flat fish that lurked on the bottom partially covered with sand waiting for food to swim by. A strike! Sandy quickly threw open the free-spool lever on the casting reel. He knew the flounder would swim away with the finger mullet before swallowing it. Sandy also gave a few soft little tugs on the line to simulate the mullet's trying to get away.

After about thirty seconds, he set the hook. It was a big one. Just like the big red, this monster was stripping the line off the reel. "Okay, Mr. Flat Guy. You're mine. Come on home to Papa." Sandy had a habit of talking to his fish when he caught one. Finally, the flounder began to tire out, and Sandy started getting line back on the spool of his bait-casting reel. Holding the rod with one hand above his head, Sandy scooped the fish out of the water with the landing net he held in the other.

When he dropped the flounder on the deck of the boat, it flapped like crazy. Furiously flapping its tail, the big fish threw itself up in the air and landed back down in rapid succession. It sounded like a machine gun going off. Finally, when it tired, Sandy pulled the hook out. The flounder was a beauty. It was around two feet long and close to a foot across.

Sandy was always amazed at how peculiar these fish looked with both eyes migrated to one side that actually became the top of the fish. It was another of nature's marvels in that it allowed the creature to lie partially buried flat on the bottom with only its swiveling eyes sticking out, lurking there until food swam by when it would blast out and seize it. Flounder were also very good to eat. He tossed it into the cooler with the red.

Sandy hooked another finger mullet on his line and cast it back out. A couple of casts later, he had another flounder in the boat, but it was not as large as the first. He added it to his slowly-filling cooler of fish. Since his father was a commercial fisherman, Sandy would be able to sell whatever fish he didn't wish to keep to Mr. Roland. This way, he always had gas money for his Evinrude. He baited up and cast out once more.

As the afternoon wore on, Sandy slowly filled the cooler with fish. He had caught a couple more reds also, which he couldn't keep, and had to throw back. Around four that afternoon, he decided to head back to Mr. Roland's dock and pulled up the anchor. Sandy wasn't in any hurry crossing back over the river to the docks. He was in his own element, and he savored the moment. The sea breeze had picked up, and there was a slight chop on the water.

Sandy saw an osprey hovering thirty feet over the water near the shallows on the south side of the Coast Guard Station. He knew it had spotted a fish. And as he expected, it tucked its wings and plummeted down toward the unsuspecting sea creature. Just before crashing into the water, the big sea-eagle spread its wings again, slowing the fall and snatched the fish from the water with its razor sharp talons, then flapped back into the air again, holding the fish.

It was another marvel of nature. Sandy wondered how the fish eagle knew to hold the fish with its head pointed forward to keep it from being a burden to fly with. If the fish were held sideways to the wind, it would have produced drag. The osprey got its feathers wet when it captured the fish, and Sandy watched as the big bird literally shook off in mid flight then kept on flying.

Out Back eased up to Mr. Roland's fish house before returning to the mooring dock. An employee Sandy knew, Clyde King, handed a fish box down to him. He unloaded eight nice-sized flounder into it and handed it back up to Clyde. He decided to keep the red for supper. "Thanks, Clyde. Mr. Roland'll put these on my Dad's account for me. How 'bout it buddy? Gas money for me."

Clyde liked Sandy. Actually, everybody in Mayport liked him. He was an uncomplicated and totally honest young man. His habits were good, and he never showed off or lied. Sandy was a child of the earth, growing into manhood. "Hey, Sandy, how come you ain't in school? Whatcha' doin', skippin'? Ya' should know bettern' that."

"Naw, Clyde, this fat bozo tried to bully me, and I got the better of him in a fight. Mr. Reynolds had to suspend me for it. You can tell I'm sufferin' bad from the punishment."

Clyde chuckled. "That'd be Bill Reynolds. He's one of us. I'll bet he hated to suspend you."

"Probably not. Mr. Reynolds knew he just sent me fishin'. I like him a lot, and I respect him. He's a real man, and he understands us. I knew I'd trapped him into his decision. My dad knew too. So this afternoon instead of college prep, I went to the school of hard knocks prep, probably a better school anyway, don't cha' think?"

Clyde grinned. He liked the School-of-Hard-Knocks statement. "Yep, I agree with you. You were involved with the real world this afternoon, and by the looks of this box, you scored an 'A' on your test."

Sandy grinned at this statement. "You know, Clyde, you're right. I guess I did get an 'A' today. Ha! Go figure. Okay, buddy, I gotta' get back to the dock. See ya." He put the outboard in gear again and pulled away from Mr. Roland's dock.

When Sandy finished tying up the *Out Back,* he lifted the cooler and his gear into the red wagon he used to cart them back and forth from the house. There was a wooden fish-cleaning station on the bank by the seawall, and he pulled the wagon over to it. His knife was razor sharp, and Sandy was superb at cleaning fish. He had the fillets slipped off of the ribs and skinned in no time, and he put the meat in a plastic bag and returned it to the cooler. He kept the red and one large flounder. Sandy recycled the carcasses of the fish by throwing them into the river for the crabs and other creatures to eat, then rinsed off his knife and the cleaning table.

Sandy's father arrived home at six o'clock that evening, washed up, and sat down at the dinner table with the rest of the family. He started dishing up his plate and looked up at Sandy. "Ya had a pretty good day today, huh son? When I dropped my catch off at Roland's, Matt told me you got a $70 credit for the fish you brought him. At least you'll have gas money for a while. You're goin' out with me tomorrow, so ya' best get to bed early. We'll get up at 4:30."

CHAPTER V – GRACIE

Friday evening, his mother told him and his father Mr. Reynolds had phoned. He said that it was Friday and that Sandy had been on suspension for two and a half days. He was releasing him from suspension, and he should return to school on Monday. Sandy had mixed emotions about that. His little vacation was suddenly shortened a day. He would have loved to spend another day in the *Out Back.*

On Monday, as was his habit, he walked out on the dock over the little lake in front of Mayport Middle School and watched the turtles and fish that swam under it. Sandy brought several slices of stale bread from home, and he broke off little pieces, balled them up and dropped them into the water. Soon he had a whole aquarium of creatures swimming beneath him. The red-eared slider turtles were especially enjoyable for him to watch. They looked like swimming painted helmets as they comically paddled back and forth with their big webbed feet. They had their little striped heads held up out of the water expectantly, competing with the fish for the balls of bread.

"You're Sandy, aren't you?"

The feminine voice startled him, and he straightened up and turned around. Hardly any of the other students ever spoke to him. She was about the prettiest girl he had ever seen. She was slightly taller than he was, which was normal for kids their age, and her golden hair fell in ringlets past her shoulders. She had on a soft blue blouse, which was tucked in neatly pressed navy blue shorts. Her eyes were as blue as the skies over the waterway, and she had a cute little turned-up nose. "I'm Gracie Allen." She held out her hand.

Sandy knew absolutely nothing about girls. The closest he had ever gotten to one was his mother, and he didn't have sisters. He blushed bright red. He didn't understand the feelings that were suddenly going on inside of his brain. Sandy grinned, reached out and gently shook the soft hand. "Er, ahm, ah, yeah, I'm Sandy. Ah, ahm nice ta' meet cha', Gracie." Gracie walked over to the rail and looked down at the creatures Sandy had chummed up.

"Oh, look at the cute little turtles! They are so funny. Can I drop a piece of bread to them?"

Sandy handed her the half slice of bread he had left. "Tear off little pieces and ball them up first." Gracie followed Sandy's suggestion and was delighted when a big soft-shell turtle with its long neck and yellow striped, pointed nose swam quickly over and grabbed a bread ball.

"Ooh, look at that one! What kind is he?"

"Oh, that's a soft-shell. They are very thin and swim very fast. The others are red-eared sliders."

"What kind of little fish are those?"

"Bream and bluegills, mostly. There are a few fingerling bass, also."

"This is one of the neatest things I've ever seen." Gracie looked up from the scene below and into Sandy's eyes. "I've never heard you talk much Sandy."

"I guess I don't have much to say." Sandy was calming down now as he got used to the lovely creature talking to him.

"I saw what you did to that ugly brute who was picking on you last Wednesday. Good. The big bully deserved what he got. He always says bad things to me. He says nasty things about my body." Gracie shuttered. "Ugh! Even the thought of that greasy, ugly monster is disgusting."

"I'm sorry he says those things to you, Gracie."

The bell signifying the beginning of the school day rang, and Gracie turned back to Sandy. "Sandy, wanna meet here again tomorrow morning? I'll bring some bread."

It was time for Sandy's cheeks to turn red again. "Sure. I'll see ya'." Their homerooms were in different directions so they parted. Sandy couldn't help it. After he had walked a few yards, he turned and looked back after Gracie as if to make sure this was really happening to him. He watched a few seconds as the beautiful head of bobbing blond curls disappeared into a crowd of students.

For the first time in his life, Sandy's mind wasn't on boats, fish, or the water. Sandy was unsure as to the feelings he was having. It was almost like being dizzy. The confusion was baffling, and there was an urgency that he didn't understand building within him. He didn't hear a word the teacher was saying.

"Sandy! Sandy, I just asked you to read the next paragraph. You don't know where we are, do you? What on earth are you thinking about? You've already been gone two days." Miss Wells was standing at the front of the class behind her podium with one hand on her hip.

The other students began to giggle, and Sandy flushed bright red. It always delighted the others when someone got on Sandy. He wasn't very popular. "Er, ahm, er, no, maam."

"No, maam what?"

"I don't know where we are. I'm sorry."

"Turn to page seventy-three, and read the paragraph that starts off the page."

Still blushing, Sandy turned to the proper paragraph and began to read. "Plants are green because they have chloroplasts . . ."

Although he tried to keep up a semblance of staying up with the other students as they read, his mind was still places he didn't understand. It would be like that the rest of the day. It was lunchtime, and Sandy would eat with Dixie Thomas' class. He went through the serving line. All the cafeteria ladies liked him. Sandy was always sure to talk to them and tell them how nice they looked. It was something his mother had taught him to do. He was brought up to respect adults. Also, Sandy had a plan. In return for the complements, Sandy received large helpings of food, which was a popular thing with him. He might be small, but he had a voracious appetite.

Sandy found a seat at the end of one of the long tables, set down his tray and opened his milk carton, and inserted a straw. Students were still coming in, and he was one of the first ones seated. Like most middle school students, lunch was one of his favorite times of the day even though Sandy usually sat alone. "Anyone sitting here?"

Sandy almost dropped his fork. The voice. It was her. For the third time that day, Sandy would experience the flush of blood rushing to his cheeks. He swallowed a huge mouthful of mashed potatoes and gravy. "Ah, er, ahm." He felt so stupid. He couldn't get his mouth to work right. "Ah, no. I mean, no, nobody's sitting there."

"Do ya' mind if I sit with you?"

"Er, ah, no, I mean yes, I mean yeah, go ahead and have a seat."

He couldn't believe his eyes as the beautiful girl who had a huge grin on her face sat down across from him, golden curls bobbing on slender shoulders as she did. And again, strange feelings were coming over him. He had never felt this way in his life. He seemed so nervous and confused inside. He wanted to talk, but he couldn't think of anything to say. He loved to look at her. Gracie was the prettiest girl he had ever seen in his life, and she had come over and asked to sit next to him. He had never even liked girls before. He always thought they were silly and that the boys who chased them around were stupid.

Gracie bit the corner of the cellophane container which held a plastic knife and fork, a napkin, a packet of salt, and another of pepper, and tore it open. Her eyes stayed on Sandy's face the whole time. "So Sandy, what'cha you into?"

"Excuse me?"

"You know, what kinda stuff do you like to do?"

"My boat. I like my boat and being out on the water."

"You have your own boat? Wow, I love boats. Will you take me for a ride sometime? My dad used to have a boat, but he sold it. I really miss being on the water."

"Sure. I'll take you for a ride whenever you want."

"What kind is it?"

"It's a nineteen foot fisherman's deep V with a hundred horsepower Evinrude on it. I keep it in Mayport at one of Mr. Roland's docks. My dad lets me take it out whenever I want, and I can go anywhere I decide to. Usually I catch fish to sell to Mr. Roland, so I can buy gas for it. When I got kicked out of school for fighting, I went fishing and made seventy dollars. You wanna' go out in the boat this Sunday?" Suddenly he realized what he had just said, and the fourth blush of the day flushed his cheeks. He hadn't blushed or talked this much in his whole life. This was almost more than Sandy had spoken in several days. Like his father, he didn't speak much. For some reason now, however, he felt like a magpie. What in the world was happening to him?

Gracie was taking tiny little bites of her food. Unthinkingly, Sandy was wolfing his down like he hadn't eaten in a week. She set her fork down and wiped her lips with the paper napkin. "I'd really like to go with you. I gotta ask my parents first though."

"Tell them it'll be safe. I have plenty of life jackets, and we'll just run around in the river and on the waterway. You can tell me tomorrow. Here, let me take your tray up to the garbage bin for you."

"Sandy, you're so thoughtful. It's really neat to have a new friend. My teacher is here to pick up her class. Gotta go. I'll talk to you later."

Sandy was confused again. As he walked toward the trash bin, he was floating on air. He hated it that they had to leave each other again. He had never experienced feelings like he was having. And the thought that Gracie might go with him in his boat excited him. Rarely did anyone go in his boat with him. He had always been pretty much a loner. Sandy was truly a chip off the old block, and almost a carbon copy of his father. Mrs. Thomas appeared at the door and her students walked over and lined up for the walk back to the class.

That was pretty much it the rest of the day for Sandy. He fantasized about Gracie and him being on the boat together and how he would show her how manly he was and how good he could handle his boat. He thought about how he would show her all the creatures and the beautiful scenery of the river and waterway he knew so well. He had never thought of the word girlfriend with respect to himself. Now he was in awe of the thought. A vision of Gracie was the last thing that passed through his mind before he drifted to sleep that night.

Five miles away in a posh, beachfront home, Gracie was lost in thought as well. She had done a daring thing when she introduced herself to Sandy. She didn't know what had gotten in to her. She was pretty much disgusted with the boys her age. They did stupid things and made awful statements to her. Others walked around with their chests filled with false pride because they were a football player or a basketball star. They treated girls like property.

She had watched Sandy for some time now. He was always quiet, and he minded his own business. Gracie also thought Sandy was very good looking. She liked the manly, rugged way he looked. There was also a mystery about him. He didn't respond to girls like the other boys did. That caused her to be interested even more. It made her sad the way other students talked bad about Sandy. They just didn't know him. They called him stuck-up and burr-head behind his back, and they said he stunk like fish.

Then came the fight. She was standing in the hall when Bart began to call Sandy names and taunt him. Gracie just knew Bart was about to hurt Sandy, and she was afraid for him. Then Sandy pulled the bravest move she had ever seen when he had the guts to attack a fellow almost twice his size. And he hurt Bart bad, too. Then he had picked up his books, calmly and fearlessly looked in everyone's eyes, and walked off. It was just too cool. *I wonder if he likes me. He sure looks at me like he does. Momma said I could go on his boat with him Sunday. I can't wait. He's different than anyone I've ever met. He doesn't show off or say stupid things. Actually, he doesn't say much at all. I really like him.*

Sandy awoke with a start the next morning. He suddenly remembered he was supposed to meet Gracie by the lake. He jumped out of bed and headed for the shower. Even though the school was a short distance from Mayport, the bus ride seemed endless. Sandy squirmed in his seat, anxious to get to the school. He had several slices of bread in a plastic bag he carried with his books.

Finally, the *yellow hound*, which is what the kids called the bus, turned off of Mazano Road into the tree branch covered circular bus unloading area behind the school. Even though he was supposed to stay seated, Sandy jumped up before the bus stopped and started for the door. He resisted the urge to run as he walked across the campus. When he emerged from the passageway between the buildings, Sandy could see the dock was empty.

He set his books down on the edge of the platform and walked out on the dock with his bread. He rolled up a few balls and dropped them in which caused the creatures to begin collecting under the dock then started rolling up balls and dropping them back in the plastic bag. *I'll have a whole bag of bread balls all ready for Gracie to drop in. I'll bet she'll like that.*

One of the largest soft shell turtles Sandy had ever seen swam up to the dock. He was amazed. Creatures always captured Sandy's attention, especially ones like this giant turtle. He had no idea a little lake like this could hold a leviathan so big. *Must be the lack of natural predators like alligators.* Its carapace was larger than a manhole cover, and its neck was as long as a man's arm. He had momentarily forgotten about Gracie as this new sight in the lake mesmerized him. "Something must be mighty interesting down there from the way you're looking."

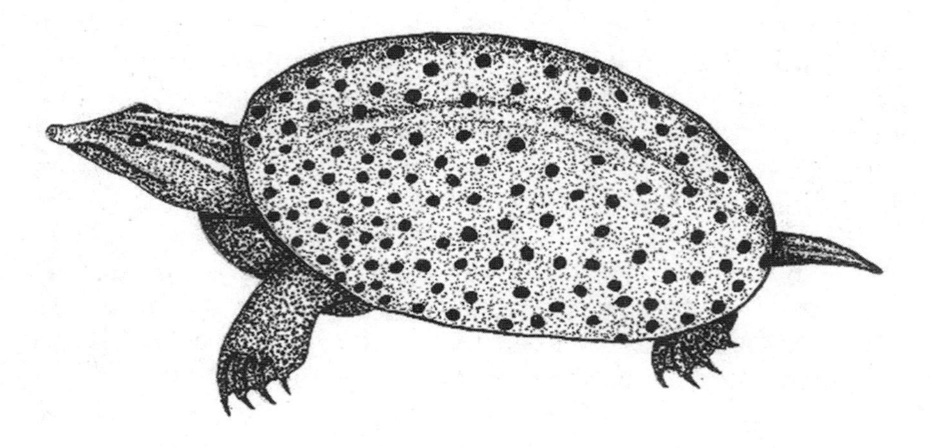

Sandy felt her arm against his as she came up next to him and leaned over the railing to see what he was looking at. "Holy cow! Look at that giant turtle. What did you call them—*soft shell*? He's huge."

"Hi, Gracie. You snuck up on me again. You must be part Indian or somethin'. Here. Take this bag of bread balls and drop some to him."

"I brought some too." She handed him a half loaf still in the bread bag.

"Dang, you sure did bring some bread. We'll attract a school of piranhas with this much bread. I'll ball it up." Sandy's statement brought a giggle out of Gracie's throat. And she started dropping balls of bread into the lake. The abundant food caused a huge stir beneath the dock as the creatures darted around wildly eating the bread balls. They were actually churning up the surface as they competed for the food.

Attracted by the commotion beneath the surface, a huge blue heron flapped down on giant wings and landed on the bank by the edge of the dock. The kids looked up in awe as it landed. It was at least four feet tall, and it was a beautiful creature.

Many of the birds in this civilized area had gotten quite used to humans, and often fishermen would throw them small fish or scraps from the fish they were cleaning. Sandy lowered his voice to a whisper. “Hold still, Gracie. I think he’s gonna catch a fish.”

Just after the words left his mouth, the giant bird plunged his long neck all the way up to its shoulders into the water then emerged with a bream the size of a man’s hand wedged between its long, scissors-like beak. It tossed the fish around so the head was pointing to him, turned its beak skyward, and shook its head so the fish would slide down his throat. The kids could see the impression of the fish as it moved down the long throat. Then it turned its attention back to the fish underneath the surface again. A small gasp emanated from Gracie’s throat. She was talking quietly. “I don’t believe what I just saw. How can it swallow something that big?

I've never seen anything like that in my life. Look, there he goes again."

The big, gray bird speared another fish and repeated the whole process again. Sandy pointed to the other end of the lake. "Gracie, this is our day. Look over there at those two otters." Two small otters had just entered the little lake through the algae covered drainage canal on the north end across from the dock.

The dark brown creatures undulated their long slender bodies animatedly while they paddled with their webbed feet, which caused them to move fluidly through the water. Sandy threw a handful of bread balls into the water beneath them. Attracted by the commotion the fish and other creatures were making, the otters submerged and swam beneath the water under the dock. The amazed kids watched as one of them captured a fish in its mouth, swam out to the middle of the lake, rolled on its back and began to eat the fish, holding it in its little webbed paws.

They didn't see the other otter catch the fish, but it emerged beside the first with one in its mouth also. A lot of the other kids had spotted the otters and as word spread, they lined the banks of the lake talking loudly and pointing at the little creatures. This was too much for the big heron, and it flapped its giant wings and took off for a quieter place.

The dock was full of kids now too. They were jabbering and pointing at the turtles and fish Sandy and Gracie had chummed up. Sandy didn't like to be amid the noisy group of kids, some who were running around and punching each other. "Come on, Gracie, let's go over by the building where it's quieter."

He picked up their books from the corner of the dock, and they walked over to the building. Gracie was chattering excitedly about what they had just witnessed, and Sandy was listening quietly. There was a concrete bench between the two buildings, and they took a seat on it. Gracie put her hand on Sandy's arm. He was surprised at the pleasure that gave him.

"Oh, I got so excited I forgot to tell you, Sandy. My mom said I could go with you on your boat Sunday. At first she said no. She said a young lady had no business being out alone with a boy running around in a boat. I reminded her that it is the 2000's ya' know, and I am fourteen. And I told her you are a very nice and polite person. Finally she gave in, but on Sunday she wants to meet you first."

"Hey, that's great. Tell you what—try to be at the dock by nine Sunday morning. That way we'll be able to enjoy the best part of the day. Bring whatever you want to eat or drink. I'll have ice."

"Where do I go?"

"My boat is docked just a little ways past Monty's Marina. There's a little empty building there and a small dirt parking lot. You can't miss it. I'll keep an eye out for your car."

Once again the morning bell spoiled their meeting, and the students filed into the building from all directions. One thousand, two hundred students entering all at once formed quite a throng of young bodies. Sandy stood up and handed Gracie's books to her. "I'll see ya' later, Gracie." He started off toward his homeroom.

"Bye Sandy."

Gracie had just entered the main doors to the building when Mary Alice Gooding came up next to her on the ramp that led into the main building. "Hi ya', Gracie girl. Whatcha' doin' hangin' around with fish man? Don't that smell of fish get to ya'?"

Gracie's cheeks flushed with anger. "Mary Alice, first, you should mind your own business. Second, it isn't any of your business what I do. Sandy is the best boy in this school, and he doesn't smell like fish. You need to get a life."

Oooh, ain't we uppity. Everybody else thinks he smells like fish, and he acts like he hates the world and everyone else. Plus, it looks like he cuts his hair with a chain saw."

"You don't know him. Just because he is quiet and keeps to himself, doesn't mean he hates everybody. If you got to know him, you would like him, too. I've got to get to class. Don't ever talk bad about him to me again." With that, Gracie stormed off down the hall to homeroom.

Sandy's route took him past the little lake once again. The big heron had returned, and the little otters had disappeared. He grinned. It was a good omen to experience events like these with nature. The day would be a good one. He would start out with PE right after Mrs. Wells' homeroom period. That meant more time out of doors.

CHAPTER VI – THE BEAST RETURNS

Bart Jenkins' three days punishment was over, and he had returned, although sporting two rather embarrassing black eyes. While Sandy was changing his clothes in the dressing room, he could see him talking to several boys in the corner. Sandy didn't need any more trouble, so he hurried into his shorts, tee shirt and sneakers and left the locker room. Mrs. Moss' PE class would meet in the football stadium, which was across a large field two hundred yards west of the school building.

The classes were playing flag football these days, and it was a game Sandy really liked because he was so agile and fast. It was hard for players from the other team to get the flags pulled from his belt. He had a seat in the bleachers with the other members of the class so Mrs. Moss could take roll.

Bart's days at home were completely different from Sandy's. His brute of a father had sent him to his room and forced him to be confined there except for having to mow and rake the lawn, wash dishes, weed the garden, and perform a host of other unpleasant chores. He had heard over and over how his father was ashamed that his son got his butt kicked by someone half his size and that he had better "make that right."

The two boys Bart was speaking with weren't any better than he was. They had failed grades also, and were troublemakers. One named Jose DeArcos was a big greasy-looking kid with long jet-black hair, a flat nose, dark skin, and a big hoop earring in one ear. Jose had tattooed his own arm with a picture of a marijuana leaf and the words *Bad Weed* written under it.

The other boy had already spent time in juvenile detention for breaking and entering. His name was Butch Mason, and he was as tall as Bart and as fat too. Butch was always dirty. His disheveled matt of brown hair looked as if a comb had never tamed it. He had a nose ring in one nostril and always smelled of sweat and body odor.

None of the three would change clothes for PE, being satisfied with the 'F' instead. Since they didn't dress out, they wouldn't be allowed to participate—a fact that suited the two fat boys perfectly well. They had to stand with all of the other non-dressers against the side of the small stadium's wall. They kept talking and looking in Sandy's direction. At first it bothered him, but as the game started, he quickly forgot about it.

Although he wasn't popular with the other students and was mostly a loner, the flag football field was one place all of this was different. Sandy was always one of the first players picked when sides were chosen. Although he wasn't very big, he was extremely fast and quick. His small size made it possible for him to turn on a dime and elude the players who were trying to snatch his flags from his belt.

The football coach had seen him play and tried to enlist him for the team, but Sandy preferred his afternoons in *Out Back* instead. Anyway, he was still pretty small to be playing with boys who were over six feet tall. Thirty-five minutes later, it was time to return to the locker room to "dress in."

As usual, Sandy walked alone up the path toward the gym. He had walked over to the water fountain behind the bleachers to get a drink and was the last one coming in. The path curved through a stand of pine trees, beyond the tennis courts, and behind the doors to the football locker rooms. He had just walked past the walled entryway to the football equipment room when Jose and Butch jumped out behind him and grabbed him by both of his arms.

Sandy struggled like a wildcat but to no avail. The two big boys were too strong. "Lemme go, damn you guys. Let go of me."

Jose just laughed. He moved his greasy, pimpled face close to Sandy's. Sandy about choked on the awful halitosis of Jose's breath. "Hey, leetel burro, ju tink ju perty tough, no? Ju go sucker keeking our freend en de nuts, and ju tink ju gonna get way wid it, no? Eeets ju turn now." Butch was laughing too. "Yeah, ya little fart. You cheated. Let's see how you like the shoe bein' on the other foot." Sandy was about to choke from the smell of this guy.

Then Bart stepped out of the darkened doorway. The leer on his face was accompanied by a drool of spittle out of the left side of his grinning mouth. He was smacking his right fist into the open palm of his left hand. "Okay, ya' little sissy. First you kick me in the nuts like a coward, then you hit me in my nose and blacken my eyes so everyone can laugh at me and my father gets mad at me. Your turn, fish bait."

Bart swung his fist into Sandy's stomach as hard as he could. Although it hurt, Sandy had a stomach of iron so it wasn't bad. Bart's next swing landed his fist on Sandy's left cheekbone, which rocked his head sideways. Bart was on a roll.

Jose was jabbering. "Heet 'em, heet 'em ageen, mon. Tha's da way, Bart."

Bart was aglow with all of his bullying mania. Blood lust had overtaken him. This was just how he liked his odds. He thought of the bloody nose and the black eyes. Bart's father's words flew through his head again. *You better make this right.* His next swing landed on Sandy's nose, which broke it instantly and threw his head back. The blow, plus the fact Sandy's arms had become slippery with sweat, caused the two bullies to lose their grip on him, and he fell to the ground.

All three bullies began to kick Sandy as he curled up in a fetal position. Crack. A fist landed on bone, and a body fell next to Sandy on the ground. It was Jose. The kicking had stopped, and Sandy looked up to see two of his African American friends fighting with Bart and Butch. Jose was out cold.

Ken Boston and Johnny Bryant Jr. were two of Sandy's closest friends at the school. Johnny's father worked on the docks for Mr. Roland. Ken's father was a mate on the *My Three Sons* shrimp boat. Sandy always joked with them and called them his AfrAm Buddies. They were both tackles on the football team and eighth graders. They were huge. Ken connected a powerful right to Bart's jaw, and two teeth popped out of his mouth like a couple of Chiclets and fell to the sidewalk. Bart fell to the ground in a crumpled heap. It hadn't been a good couple of weeks for him. Butch took a huge swing at Johnny who caught his arm, threw his hip into him and swung him in a judo throw through the air. He landed against the wall of the gym. Butch's arm got caught beneath him as he fell, breaking it. He screamed. Bart was crying again.

Sandy had gotten up and he took off his tee shirt and held it against his nose to stop the bleeding. Everybody was breathing hard. Ken turned to Sandy. "Sandy, you okay? You took a pretty good lick to the nose there, man. 'Fraid you're gonna' have a couple black eyes too."

"Yeah, guys, I'm alright. I just need to get this bleeding stopped. Man, am I glad you guys came along. I saw them planning this thing, and I should have paid more attention." The red welts on Sandy's sides were starting to darken where he had received kicks from the bullies.

Johnny pointed at them. "Those hurt? You are gonna have some pretty heavy black and blues. I told Ken I saw those three pigs plotting together and nodding at you. I knew they were up to something. Then when I didn't see 'em in the locker room and you weren't there either, I told him we needed to go find you. And it's lucky we did too. I sent Bill Croup to find Ms. Moss and tell her."

Jose groaned and started to wake up. Butch was holding his arm and limping toward the locker room. Bart was holding his face and crying. Just then Ms. Moss and Mr. Reynolds came around the building. They both had concerned looks on their faces, which deepened when they saw the two boys on the ground, Butch limping away holding his arm and Sandy mopping his face with a bloody tee shirt.

Mr. Reynolds hurried up to Sandy, Johnny, and Ken. "What in the world's happened here?"

Ken pointed at Bart. "Crybaby there put these two dummies up to holding Sandy while he punched him. Then they got him on the ground and started kicking him. Johnny saw them planning it, and we came looking for Sandy. They were beating him up pretty bad when we got here, and then they tried to take us on. I guess they thought three against two were pretty good odds. They weren't though."

Officer Jerrell came around the building and walked up to the group of students and adults. "What's goin' on? It doesn't look too good to me." Mr. Reynolds pointed at Sandy. "We have a serious battery on Sandy Stevens by those three. I want them arrested. They won't be coming back here. They're going to the alternative school. We got one with a broken arm, so he'll need immediate medical attention first. Can you call an emergency vehicle for me? We'll need the other two looked at as well."

Officer Jerrell used his portable radio to call for the emergency personnel. Jose sat up and was holding his head when Officer Jerrell helped him to his feet and handcuffed him. Next Officer Jerrell looked over to Bart. "Bart, get up off of the ground and quit crying. Your bullying days at this school are over. Pick up those two teeth and put 'em in your pocket. They may be able to stick 'em back in your head."

Bart did as he was told, and Officer Jerrell handcuffed him as well. He looked at Sandy. "You okay, son? Looks like they got you pretty good. You'll have a couple of nice shiners tomorrow."

"Yes, sir, I'm okay. If Johnny and Ken hadn't come when they did, I wouldn't be okay, though. I need to go change clothes and wash up."

Mr. Reynolds looked at Ms. Moss. "You better get back to your class. We'll take care of everything here. Sandy, do I need to phone anybody for you? Do you want the medics to look you over?"

"No, sir. I'll be fine once I wash up. I'm gonna just throw this gym shirt away. It ain't no good anymore."

News of the fight flew around the school like wild fire. Gracie was utterly shocked when she heard about Sandy's beating by the three bullies. She looked for him in the hall between classes, but he wasn't there. That increased her anxiety. Mr. Reynolds had insisted that the emergency medical technicians take a look at Sandy also to be sure he wasn't injured.

Butch was taken to the hospital, and Officer Jerrell took Jose and Bart to the Juvenile Detention Center. Bart's father was called by Officer Jerrell and told that he needed to pick Bart up from the JDC and take him to a dentist. He had his mouth rearranged to match his nose and eyes. Obadiah Jenkins knew better than to test his luck by losing his temper with Officer Jerrell, so he remained quiet. Officer Jerrell had one more thing to say. "You know, Mr. Jenkins, if I can prove you put your son up to this, I'm going to have you arrested for child abuse. Good-bye, sir."

Obadiah Jenkins held the phone out, looking at it. He started to really worry now. It was entirely possible that blubbering son of his would crack and tell all he knew. *Arrested!* He slowly lowered the receiver and replaced it in the cradle. Officer Jerrell called a detective.

When the police car arrived at the detention center, a detective was waiting. Detective Barry Stevenson was an extremely tall and thin, handsome African American man. He wore a small mustache and a flat top haircut. He met Officer Jerrell at the door of the detaining cell. "Hi, Clarence. These the two you told me about?"

"Hey, Barry. Yeah, the little one's Jose, and the big guy is Bart. Why don't you start with Bart, because his dad needs to take him to the dentist as soon as he gets here." "Bart, why don't you come with me?"

Officer Jerrell unlocked the cuffs and removed them from Bart and turned to Jose. Bart followed Detective Stevenson down the hall to a little room that held a table and two chairs. "Sit down, son." Bart sat down and Detective Stevenson sat across from him. "Bart, it is important that you are completely honest with me. I'm going to ask you a few questions. Tell me what happened the first time between you and Sandy."

Bart related the story as he remembered it to Detective Stevenson who took notes and listened quietly.

"I phoned Mr. Reynolds, and he told me your father was pretty mad. Officer Jerrell had to calm him down. How was he with you when he drove you home?"

"He was real mad at me. He told me he was ashamed of me for letting a little kid beat me up and that it would embarrass him to have his friends know it. I got sent to my room and made to do hard chores for the three days." "For fighting and bullying?"

"No, for losing the fight."

"Did he say anything else?"

"Yeah, he told me I'd better 'make it right.'"

"What do you think he meant by that?"

"I don't know what you mean, sir."

"Look, Bart, you are in a heap of trouble. Your only chance is to come clean with me. There are a lot of things I can say to a judge to make it easier on you. Or, there are things I can say which can lock you up for a while. Your only chance is to tell me the truth."

Bart was terrified. "He wanted me to get Sandy back and make him pay for what he did. He said it more than once, too."

"Okay, Bart, that's all I have. Some advice for you. You are getting a pretty bad reputation, and now you will have to go before a judge. It's time to take a long, hard look at yourself son, and think about where you are headed. You pick on others because you don't feel good about yourself. It's time you change that. A fellow your size should be out for football and making a real name for yourself. It's up to you, Bart."

"Yessir, thank you."

Detective Stevenson followed Bart back down the hall and escorted Jose back to the room. "Have a seat Jose. I have a few questions for you. You were seen with Butch and Bart before the attack. What were you talking about?

"Bart, he tell us hee's papa be mad at heem 'cause de leetle boy beat heem up. He say ta' us dat hee's papa say ta' get de leedle boy back an he need us to help."

"Why would you help Bart to gang up on this little fellow? Doesn't that seem wrong to you?"

"Cause Bart, hee's my dog, man. We dogs gotta' steeck together, comprende?"

Detective Stevenson leaned over and looked Jose directly in his eyes. "Yeah, I comprende, and now you have a record for assault and battery and have to go before the judge. This'll cost your Momma some money, too. It's time for you to clean up your act, Mr. Dog. That's all I have."

Detective Stevenson took a statement from Butch when he got out of the hospital and found it to be the same thing. He had Obadiah Jenkins arrested and charged with contributing to the delinquency of a minor and child abuse. The boys were all transferred to the alternative school for wayward children who had serious disciplinary problems in their neighborhood schools.

Finally it was lunchtime. Gracie rushed in the cafeteria and found Sandy sitting by himself as usual at one of the tables. She had brought her lunch from home, so she rushed over and sat down across from him. "Oh Sandy, I'm so sorry. Did they hurt you bad? I heard all about it. Dang, look at your face."

Sandy's nose was bright red, and his eyes had started to darken. There was a huge bruise on his left cheekbone. "It'll probably hurt more tomorrow, but I'm okay. Ken and Johnny saved my butt, though. Those bums had me on the ground and all three were kicking me as hard as they could. That's okay. They're in jail now, and they'll be kicked out of Mayport. I won't have to worry about them any time soon."

"Are you sure you aren't hurt?"

"Yeah, Mr. Reynolds had the medics check me over, and I'm okay. They said my nose was fractured, but it's not serious. I'd really rather talk about something else."

"I'm sorry, Sandy. I've just been worried about you ever since I heard about it. What can we talk about?"

"Gracie, can you believe the creatures we saw this morning. I mean rarely have I seen that number of different creatures in the little lake before at the same time. Actually, I never have. Gosh, we saw a great blue heron catching fish, fish in the pond eating bread balls, a giant soft-shell, a bunch of other turtles, and a couple otters. Great. I think it's good luck to see wild creatures, and we have a bunch of it coming our way now."

The next morning, Sandy had a sore body. His torso had big blue bruises all over it, he had two big black eyes, and his nose was swollen. As he groaned and swung his legs over the side of the bed, he had to pause because the whole world looked blurry. Finally, his injured eyes became adjusted to being open. There was a crusty substance in the corner of each one of them.

Sandy stumbled to the bathroom and washed the crust out of his eyes. Next, he turned the shower on hot, and when the water started to steam, he stepped in. Sandy loved his shower in the morning, and this one in particular was medicinal. Already, he felt better as he straightened his body up and turned his face into the warm spray coming from the showerhead. When he saw the sad sight of his face in the mirror, all he could do was shake his head. He was sure to take a big ribbing from the other students today. They always looked for ways to pick on him, and this was sure to give them ammunition. *That's okay. At least none of them will call me a chicken. Three against one, and bigger boys at that! Anybody should be disgusted with that. Anyway, they all went to jail and won't be back at Mayport. Good riddance.*

After he got dressed, he walked out of his room and down to the kitchen where his father and older brother Chad sat at the table eating breakfast. His father looked up from the newspaper when he heard Sandy pull out a chair. "Damn, son, you look like a raccoon."

Chad broke out in uproarious laughter, and it was catching. Soon, Sandy, his mother, Jeanette, who was cooking bacon and eggs on the range, Chad, and his father were all laughing. "We'll have to get you a big beefsteak to put on them eyes, boy. You hurt much?"

"Yeah, Pop, I'm pretty sore, but I'm fine. At least those goats are in jailn and that punk's dad is in jail too. I think I did the school a favor. Boy, was I lucky Ken and Johnny came looking for me. Those bums would have really hurt me. As it turned out, Ken and Johnny hurt them pretty bad. I'm sure glad I don't have a father like Bart's."

Steve Stevens flashed a little smile at his son and looked back down at his paper. Jeanette walked over to Sandy and set down a steaming plate of eggs over easy, three pieces of bacon, toast, and a pile of white grits with a big, yellow, melting pat of butter in the center. Jeanette was a petite, pretty blond lady who had a nice svelte figure. "What 'cha want ta' drink, son?"

"How about some orange juice, Momma? Thanks." Jeanette turned to get the juice, and Sandy dug into his breakfast. He was starved. His mother ended up cooking him two more eggs and a couple more pieces of bacon.

As Sandy had predicted, the poking fun started as soon as he got on the school bus. But probably, more of the students were concerned about him, and they told him how tough he was to stand up to the bullies. Sandy was a good-natured kid and quietly put up with the kidding. Mostly, he was hoping nobody would make the observation his father had that the two black eyes made him look like a raccoon. That would really set everyone off.

He got lots of stares as he walked past other students on his way to the little dock on the lake after he got off of the bus. This time, Gracie had gotten there before him and was leaning over the rail, dropping bread balls down to the critters that swam in the water below. Sandy tiptoed over, goosed her on both of her sides, and stood there grinning when she straightened up and whirled around suddenly. What had been a look of anger on her face, turned to one of affection and concern when she saw it was Sandy.

"Oh, it's you. Somebody was gonna' get hit for touching me, but you're my friend, and it's okay. Oh, my. Look at your face. My poor baby. Sandy, you look like a raccoon." Gracie gasped a quick breath and put a hand over her mouth. "Oh, I'm sorry, Sandy. I shouldn't have said that. It just slipped out."

Sandy's grin never left his face. Gracie could tease him all she wanted and anyway, nobody else heard the statement. "Yeah, my Pop said the same thing, but I'm hoping that nobody else thinks of that. They'd be pretty hard on me."

Gracie put her hand on his arm. "Sandy, do you hurt? You must. Oh, that's awful."

"I guess it's not as bad as it looks. Actually my ribs where those retarded meatheads kicked me hurt more. You haven't forgotten about Sunday, have you? I'm really looking forward to showing you the waterway. You're gonna really have fun. It's beautiful out there."

"Oh, no. I can barely wait. Tell you what—I'l l make some sandwiches for you too. What kind do you like?"

"I'll eat anything. I do like mustard and mayonnaise on my sandwiches, though. And I'll have a cooler and plenty of water. I might even throw in a couple fishing poles just for fun. Maybe I can tie you into a big ol' redfish."

Just then the bell signaling the start of the day rang, and the students started filing in the doors of the school. Gracie bent down and gathered up her backpack. "Bye, Sandy. I'll see you at lunch time."

Sandy watched as Gracie walked away. He wasn't sure what he was feeling, but he liked it. It was wonderful to have a nice new friend, and especially, a girlfriend.

CHAPTER VII – THE *MIS*-ADVENTURE

Sandy was elated when the final bell rang on Friday. Two whole days of freedom awaited him and Sunday would be one of the most special of his entire life. Sandy decided to go king fishing on Saturday because his fishermen friends told him they were running at the inshore reefs. The big king mackerels were fun to catch. And there was a plenty of meat on one fish, so it would mean good gas money. It was very common to catch kings that weighed more than twenty-five pounds. He decided that chum fishing would be the best way to go after them. To slow troll with pogies took a baitwell with flowing water, which he didn't have.

His mother fried a pile of fresh Mayport shrimp along with French fries, boiled okra, and spinach. She also blackened some of the red fish and put it on the table. Sandy was tearing into the shrimp, which were one of his favorite foods, rivaling even fried chicken, rice, and gravy. Steve Stevens grinned at his son. "Boy, for a little fella', you sure can put away some groceries."

"Shrimp are my favorite. And this is the best time of the year because the catch is good. These are fresh, and they're huge." Sandy had one of his cheeks swollen with a gob of chewed shrimp.

"Ya' fishin' tomorrow, boy?"

"Yessir. I'm gonna get up at five and get on the water before the sun comes up."

"Well, catch some fish so you'll have gas money. That's part of the rules. A man's gotta' pay his own way with his labor."

Sandy went to bed early, so he would get plenty of sleep before his early wakeup time. He wouldn't need to set an alarm, because he knew he would wake up automatically. His internal clock was pretty precise, and sure enough, at five the next morning Sandy's eyes blinked open. Just as the nights before, he still had quite a bit of goo in them, but at least they weren't sore any more. His ribs were feeling better as well.

He jumped out of bed and quietly padded his way to the bathroom. His brother shared their bedroom, and it wouldn't be fair to wake him up. Sandy and Chad were very different. Sandy was small, but Chad was huge. Sandy liked freedom and the wild, open areas of nature; Chad was the athlete and played sports year round. Sandy would go out on the water, and Chad would go to track or football practice. Sandy got up early, and Chad slept in.

His father was going out fishing also, and everybody but Chad was awake. Jeanette made a huge plate of scrambled eggs, toast and bacon for everyone. The fresh coffee was invigorating to Sandy. There was something about a cup of coffee early in the morning that made it taste extra good. Characteristically, there was very little conversation as Sandy and his dad and mom ate.

Jeanette was spreading strawberry jam on a piece of toast when she looked at Sandy and pointed toward the refrigerator with her strawberry jam-covered knife. "I made you a couple sandwiches for today. They're in the fridge. Actually, I made three. I know you like Cuban's with a lot of mustard, so that's what they are."

"Thanks, Momma. I love Cuban sandwiches. Thanks."

Steve got up, pulled on his ball cap, and pushed his chair under the table. "Jeanette, I'll be back about six. Wadda' ya' say we have some steaks for supper tonight? I've been needin' me some red meat."

"Okay, honey. I'll drive up to Terry's Market and grab a few. I'll get some potatoes to mash as well."

Steve pecked Jeanette on the cheek and walked out of the door. "Be careful, boy."

Sandy stuffed his sandwiches in a plastic grocery bag and added a few bottles of water. There was already a lot of water on the boat, but he always made sure to have more than he needed. He pulled his red wagon over to the shed behind the house and loaded his fishing poles, tackle box, and a large plastic garbage can. He also threw in a burlap bag with some large, empty white bleach jugs attached to it for flotation. He had left his cooler on the boat.

The yellow light from the street lamps was punctuated with whirling black dots of the hoards of insects that buzzed around in it. The lights cast an eerie glow on the ground as Sandy pulled his wagon of fishing equipment in and out of the shadows. As he neared the docks, his sense of smell told him it was low tide.

Low tide left myriads of sea creatures exposed to the air until the waters returned at high tide. Countless carcasses of deceased fish, mollusks and crustaceans were omnipresent in the fishing village. Each, in addition to the exposed seaweed, added its aroma to the smell of a low tide.

Actually, Sandy already knew that the tide would be low because he kept up with the charts. Good fishermen always considered several natural occurrences when fishing. The tide was one. Sandy liked an incoming tide. The temperature of the water was significant, the phase and location of the moon was another factor. The presence and location of baitfish in an area was also important. The moon would be setting about the time the sun rose, which was perfect. The water was very warm around the inshore reefs, and there were lots of baitfish swimming there.

As Sandy pulled his wagon up to the seawall where *Out Back* was moored, it seemed as if every piling in Mayport had a sleeping pelican on top of it. The roofs of the fish houses all had sleeping seagulls dotting the tops of them, beaks tucked under a wing. The squawk of a large, white snowy egret echoed in the night as its ghost shape undulated past on huge, silent wings in the semidarkness. Everything was still and placid. The wind was calm, and there were no cars on Mayport Road. The entire village seemed to be softly aglow in the fuzzy yellow radiance of the streetlights. Sandy loved this time of the morning. He swatted a fat mosquito that landed on his cheek and flicked it off of his hand.

In the quiet darkness, the sounds of him getting into his boat and loading his gear reverberated loudly even though he wasn't really being noisy. In times like these, little noises became big, because there was little competition from other sounds.

The dock where Sandy's boat was tied was a short distance to where Cap'n Bill Aley's boat, *Restless*, was docked. He could see that Cap'n Bill and some others were going diving today as they were loading the gear. From where Sandy was standing down in his boat, he could see a large van pull into the parking lot and a huge man get out. He slung a couple of scuba tanks over his shoulders and started down the path for the *Restless*. Sandy recognized him when he got closer. It was Robbie Duncan. Robbie often dove with

Cap'n Bill. Sandy really admired Robbie and was amazed at his huge size and bulging muscles. That's what he wanted to look like.

"Hi there, Robbie. See y'all are goin' out today."

"Oh, hi, Sandy. I didn't see ya' down there."

"Doin' some sport diving?"

"Actually, no, a fella' sunk his Off-shore 30 near BR a couple days ago and the insurance company has hired Cap'n Bill to bring it back up. It oughta' be a lot of fun. You should go with us some time. You're old enough to take a dive course."

"Gosh, Robbie, I'd really like that. I'd love to be a diver."

"Gotta' go, Sandy. We need to get an early start. BR's a long way out, ya' know. See ya'."

"See ya', Robbie."

Robbie ambled off towards the *Restless*.

Sandy turned the key, and the Evinrude outboard coughed into life amid the usual puff of smoke. He would let the engine idle to warm it up while he loaded and stowed his gear and untied the lines from the dock.

Sandy put the engine in gear and idled down the river to Mr. Roland's fish house where he would load his cooler with ice. It was another amenity offered to his family, because they sold their catch to Roland's Seafood. When he tied up to Mr. Roland's dock, Johnny Bryant, Sr. came over pulling a box of ice behind him with a fishhook. He was the father of the Johnny who joined Ken Boston to defeat the bullies. "How you feelin', Mr. Sandy? Johnny Junior told me about them scumbags that tried to hurt you. Gotcha' a couple nice shiners, ain't ya'?"

"Mornin', Mr. Johnny. How can anyone feel bad on a beautiful morning like this, especially when he's goin' fishin'?"

"Yeah, you right there, young man. Whatcha' goin after today?"

"I heard the kings are runnin'. I thought I'd run out about nine or ten miles to the inshore reefs and try and hang into a few. Maybe I'll try Nine Mile. I can always use gas money, you know. Lotta meat in a big king fish. They got a lot of body and not much head. If I get a few, I'll have me a bunch of meat to sell. It takes a bunch of fish from the waterway or river to make me much money. Way I see it, I can make enough gas money to last me a month or two."

"Yeah, the fishermen've been bringin' us some nice kings. If I were you, though, I'd make it an early day. It's sposed to start blowin' out of the west this afternoon. Water'll chop up pretty bad. You don't want to get caught in that."

"Thanks for the information. I watched the weather on TV last night and 'ole Tim Deegan showed the front that's comin' across from Texas. That's why it's so good to get started early. I got lots of fishin' time before noon. Thanks for the ice. See ya' this afternoon."

Johnny helped Sandy shove off and watched as the boy put the boat in gear and idled out into the river, as thoughts coursed through his head. *Now that's how a young man oughta grow up. Other kids are out runnin' the streets and this boy is living a real life in his boat. I hope he ain't got too cocky taday, though. A westerly pushes ya farther from shore and cooks them waves up in your face when you turn back east to come home.*

Other kids might have been frightened or apprehensive about going out on the big ocean all alone but not Sandy. He had been going out ever since he was born. He was just as at home on the water as he was on land and maybe more so. Actually, he liked being on the water the best. He also didn't mind being alone. It wasn't that he invited the solitude; he just didn't think about asking anyone else to go along because he was usually too excited about going himself. Also, a lot of times when he had taken others, they had complained about things. One kid got seasick and vomited the entire time until Sandy could get him back to the dock. Still another tried to second guess or criticize everything that Sandy did and tried to tell him what to do. Being on the water in *Out Back* was nothing short of a religion to Sandy, and he was content to worship alone.

Sandy increased the speed once he got into the shipping channel and *Out Back* got up on a plane. It was 6:30 now, and the sky in the east was a beautiful, shimmering coral color that reflected off of the edges of the few clouds that floated above. The tide was at ebb, and the water in the river was very calm. That was great. He would be able to pick up some speed and get out to the fishing grounds quickly. He passed the carrier basin, which was south of the river and could see the colossal USS John F. Kennedy aircraft carrier towering above. It was longer than three football fields and carried over 3,000 personnel on board. It was a floating city and indeed, one that was larger than many cities in the United States.

The wind was warm in Sandy's face, made so as it picked up the temperature of the water it blew over. He was traveling along at about 40 knots, which was a pretty good pace. One knot was roughly 1.15 statute miles per hour. Since the distance a boat traveled over the bottom and the distance it traveled on the surface were different, knots were used by sailors to measure a boat's speed over water. Wind, current, waves and other factors always affected a boat's movement over the surface.

Now the large jetty rocks loomed above the surface to the north and south of him. Almost every one had a sleeping pelican, sea gull, or cormorant on it. Watching the sun rise at sea was little short of a religious experience. At first, the pink glow of the sky on the horizon started to brighten to a deep red-orange. The colors reflected off a line of clouds that hung high above the water. Then a dazzlingly, brilliant pinprick of light appeared as the first rays of sun rose above the ocean on the horizon. It was amazing how fast the sun moved when it rose. When it was overhead, it was difficult to perceive any motion, but when it rose over the horizon, it literally flew into the sky in a matter of seconds. First, there was the scintillating, coral-colored pinhead of light, then the orb floated quickly up like a glowing, red-orange balloon emerging from the dark line of ocean.

Bottle-nosed dolphins had awakened with the sun, and they were rolling past on all sides of the *Out Back*. A few began some aerial gymnastics and burst straight up out of the water, turned flips, and plunged back in nose first. The gulls and pelicans had taken wing and dotted the skies everywhere. It was a gorgeous morning.

Sandy filled his lungs with the pristine air that wafted in above the ocean. As his boat cleared the green buoy at the end of the south jetties, he spotted what he was looking for on the horizon directly east of his position—a shrimp boat. He pointed the prow of the *Out Back* towards it and headed away from shore. Sandy's father had equipped *Out Back* with a VHF radio, which was what the different vessels on the water used. This was as much for safety as it was for the convenience of contacting other skippers. Since the family also had a unit in the house, either Steve or Sandy could be contacted when they were on the water. And they could talk to each other.

Sandy picked up the microphone and turned the dial to 72. A lot of times he would leave it tuned to the emergency channel, which was 16, but most boats in the area kept it on 72. “Can I have a radio check? This is the *Out Back* calling.”

The speaker on the radio sprang into life. “Readin’ ya’ loud and clear, Cap’n. Have a good day. *Sea Dancer*, out.”

“Thank you Cap’n, for the radio check. You have a nice day too. *Out Back* out.”

It was important to always make sure the radio was working. If an emergency occurred, there wouldn’t be time to tinker around with it.

At 40 knots, it didn’t take Sandy long to close in on the shrimp boat. It was Cap’n Alpo’s *Miss Corrine*. Al Butler was a good captain and fisherman. He was very popular in Mayport. Sandy took a five-dollar bill from his pocket and stuffed it in the burlap bag that had the floats attached to it.

The *Miss Corrine* had both booms lowered on either side of her trawling for shrimp. When they were trawling, they moved extremely slow. Long cables stretched from the pulleys on either end of the booms and disappeared beneath the water behind the boat. Raucously screaming seagulls pirouetted everywhere above the boat, and many landed on the booms, roof of the cabin, and in the rigging. Pelicans sailed in and out of the hoard of seagulls. These feathered creatures were the bane of the fishermen, because they got bombarded with bird droppings from the mass of birds above. The shrimp boats were always covered with white blotches of dried bird feces.

When the shrimpers pulled in their try net and found it to be full, it would indicate that it was time to pull n the big nets that were trawled along the bottom, because they would be full of shrimp also. The nets were non-discriminatory, however, and there was always a huge amount of by-catch in the nets along with the shrimp. When the nets were hauled over the gunwales of the shrimp boat, the shrimpers would dump the contents of the net on the deck in the stern of the boat, grab a couple white buckets to sit on and start sorting through the pile of writhing, jumping creatures with short, hand-held rakes. The shrimp, crabs, and edible fish were put into wire bucket-like containers; the rest of the sea life—much of it dead by then was shoveled back overboard through the scupper holes that were at deck level and ran through the side of the hull.

Free food is what excited the birds and other sea life so much. Over the years, the birds learned to recognize signs that food was coming and to react to it. Birds weren't the only creatures inviting themselves to dine from the shrimpers' by-catches. Sharks, other fish, and dolphins would weave back and forth in the water behind the shrimp boat as well.

Sandy guided the *Out Back* between the two cables that were pulling the net behind the shrimp boat. Since the net was on the bottom forty feet down, there was no danger of fouling the prop on his outboard motor. Dolphins were rolling excitedly on both sides of his boat, circling in and out of the area between the cables and on the outsides of them. He could hear the *whoofff* as they exhaled before catching another breath and diving again.

Buddy Mims, one of Cap'n Alpo's mates, was standing at the stern of the shrimp boat that towered above the little *Out Back,* and he waved down to Sandy. Sandy was busy guiding the boat as it swirled back and forth in the current created by the giant screw, as the propeller was called, that pushed the shrimp boat. Sandy held up the mesh bag and yelled up to Buddy. "Y'all got any chum?"

Buddy was a muscular fellow with jet-black hair. He sported a mustache and goatee. Characteristically, Buddy wore fisherman's yellow rubber bib overalls, a white tee shirt, and he had a Jacksonville Jaguars ball cap on his head.

"Yeah, we just pulled the nets. That's what all these damn birds are so crazy about. Throw me your bag. Goin' after them kings, huh? Where ya plan to fish?"

Sandy heaved the bag with the bleach jugs up over the gunwales, which Buddy caught in mid-air. "Thought I'd start at Nine Mile. Buddy, put me some nice silver trout in the bag on top, okay?" There were dozens of marked fishing areas in the Atlantic Ocean between land and the *Ledge,* which was what the continental shelf was called. Flags placed there by the Jacksonville Offshore Sport Fishing Club marked many, and others were locatable only by Loran or now, GPS, which was a device that received information from satellites and gave fishermen their position at sea. The area just east of Jacksonville was known as *The Party Grounds.*

The bottom was what made a good fishing area. Creatures at the bottom of the food chain needed structure to live on. Many of them attached themselves to the structure, and others lived in or around it. Larger creatures would feed on the smaller creatures, and still larger ones would feed on those until it got to the really big ones at the end of the food chain like grouper, snapper, kingfish, dolphin (the fish or mahi mahi), wahoo, cobia, and others. Of course these were the ones preyed upon by man who devised ingenious ways to catch them. Good structure also gave some of the fish places to hide and provided shelter, which they needed to live. These fish were known as *bottom fish* as opposed to the roaming pelagic species. Thus to *bottom fish* was to stop the boat and drop the baits down to the bottom.

Trolling was the preferred method employed by other fishermen, who dragged baits behind their boats around the reef area trying to catch striking fish like kings, wahoo, and dolphin. Some fishermen did both. Another type of fishing was chum fishing, which was what Sandy intended to do

Obviously, *Nine Mile* was about nine miles away from land. Buddy lowered the bag and jugs into the boat. "If I were you, I'd run on out to *EF*. Heard there was a lot going on out there, and it's only a little farther from shore." *East Fourteen & Fifteen* were around fifteen miles from shore and almost directly east of *Nine Mile*. "You better get a early start home, though. I'm sure you checked the weather. Ole' Tim Deegan says we're in for a blow tonight. Your little ole' boat won't be much use to ya if ya get caught in that storm."

"Thanks for the information. Yeah, I saw the weather report. I'm only going to fish until noon." Sandy waved at Buddy again and eased off on the throttle so the *Out Back* slowed down, allowing the shrimp boat to pull ahead of him, and then he was free of the cables. He throttled up again and pulled alongside of the *Miss Corrine,* matching his speed with that of *Miss Corrine* so he stayed even with her. He could see Buddy bent over with a big aluminum—square point shovel filling his mesh bag with the creatures that would be his chum from the deck. When Buddy finished filling the bag, he pulled the drawstrings to close the top, lifted the heavy bag up on the gunwale and rolled it off into the water behind the shrimp boat. The bleach jugs kept the bag afloat, and the shrimp boat gradually pulled away from it.

Sandy steered the *Out Back* over to the bag and pulled it to the side of the boat with his gaff. With a great effort he dragged the soaking, hefty burlap bag over the gunwale of the boat and let it fall to the bottom. He and Buddy exchanged waves once again, and the *Out Back* was underway towards *EF*.

Like *Nine Mile*, *EF* was almost due east from the Sea Buoy that marked the entrance to the shipping channel that led to the jetties of the St. Johns River. Although Sandy had a small hand-held GPS, he really didn't need it, because both *Nine Mile*, which he would pass on the way, and *EF* were marked by flags. The three feet long triangular black flags hung from long fiberglass poles. The poles were supported by Styrofoam floats that were anchored to the bottom. The flags marked the area of the reefs, not a particular reef itself. Sandy would use his boat's compass to steer by. Since he would be out of sight of land and there were no landmarks, the compass would guide him.

EF consisted of at least ten different reef sites that were in the same general vicinity. He was hoping the big king fish were cruising around in the area trying to feed on the schools of fish that lived above the reefs. He passed the *Nine Mile* flag, which indicated to him he only had about six more miles to go. Sandy spotted the *EF* flag long before he got close to it. His eagle sharp eyes picked it up on the horizon not long after he passed *Nine Mile.* He had guided his boat almost directly to it. Sandy could see that there were four other boats already fishing in the area, which was a good sign. That meant that the fish were probably here as well. It was also nice to have other boats in the area should one develop engine or boat problems. One boat appeared to be bottom fishing, and the other three were slow trolling with pogies. Sandy knew that a pogie was another name for menhaden that were small, silver colored, flat fish. They were excellent bait. Pogies were slow-trolled alive. Their shiny silver sides flashed brightly in the sunlight, attracting striking fish. Sandy steered *Out Back* clear of the other boats, upstream from them. He wanted his chum to drift away from the other fishermen.

When he found the spot where he wanted to fish, Sandy slowed his engine down and turned it off. He had a home-made sea anchor, which consisted of a four-foot square of canvas attached at each corner by a piece of polyethylene rope. The four ropes led out to where they were braided to one, and the single rope was tied to the bow cleat on the starboard gunwale. Sandy threw the sea anchor overboard where it ballooned out like a parachute against the current. Then he turned the outboard motor so that the foot made the boat swing out in the current against the pull on the sea anchor. The combination of sea anchor and water flowing past the foot of the outboard helped him keep his boat drifting sideways to the current, so he could fish from the side of the boat rather than the bow or the stern.

Sandy dumped the contents out of the chum bag into the garbage can that sat on the deck of the boat. He had two seven-foot long fiberglass fishing poles that he would use. Each had Shimano reels on them spooled with 30 pound test monofilament line. Sandy knew that kingfish were smart. He couldn't use heavy line, because they could see it and wouldn't take the bait. He had made some *king rigs* which were attached to the lines on each pole. They consisted of six feet of brown stainless steel leader wires that ran through three corks spaced a foot and a half apart. On the end of each was a large, brown 4/0 treble hook.

Quickly, Sandy sorted through the chum. It was already starting to stink. He selected two foot and a half long, silver trout and slit the stomachs open with a knife. He knew the shiny silver sides of the trout would attract the fish he wanted to catch. Into each, he slid a long piece of Styrofoam and wired the cavities shut around them. He hooked one to each of his treble hooks and let the baits out so they drifted out in the current from the boat. The Styrofoam kept the silver trout on the surface of the water. The corks on the wire leader kept it floating on the surface as well. He let one line out longer than the other so his baits were spaced apart. Both rods were stuck into the pole holders on the starboard gunwale of the boat.

Then he took several handfuls of the dead creatures from the chum bucket and threw them overboard. They drifted away from the boat. Some of it sank and some floated on the surface. He took a syringe with a large needle from his tackle box. He began to select fish from the chum, and he stuck each one with the needle and inflated it with air, then threw it into the water. This caused the dead fish to float on the surface where his baits were. Soon, he had a stream of floating chum that led out from the boat and past the silver trout baits that floated on the surface.

Sandy wiped his hands on his shorts, grabbed one of the Cuban sandwiches and a bottle of water from the cooler and sat down on the bench seat to wait. Although Sandy didn't wear a watch, judging by the height of the sun, it was around nine in the morning. He also continued to inflate a few fish and throw them and some handfuls of chum overboard every few minutes. It was important to keep the chum line intact.

He had just taken the last bite of his sandwich when he saw some action in his chum line. About one hundred yards away, a splash on the surface indicated a fish had taken some chum and was following his chum line in towards his bait. Then there was another closer in, and then there was another, and then another. Sandy set his water bottle down and got ready to man a pole. The feeding fish was following the chum line to the silver trout furthest out. He quickly reeled in the pole that had the silver trout nearest to the boat. A hook up could lead to a tangle up if the line was still out. Then he pulled the canvas sea anchor into the boat. When he had a hook-up, he would not be able to get it out of the way and still fight the fish.

The silver trout on Sandy's hook was quite a bit larger than the other creatures in the chum. Plus, the shiny silver scales reflected brightly in the water, just the thing to attract an aquatic predator. The water exploded where the silver trout floated, and the reel's alarm clicker started whirring as line was being stripped from it. Something big had taken the bait.

Sandy grabbed the pole from the pole holder and slid the button that disengaged the clicker to an off position. The tip of the pole was bent in a tight arc, and he strained against the pull on the line. He had set his star drag light so the strike of the fish wouldn't break his line. He tightened it down a little which slowed down the rate his line was being stripped from the reel. The drag was a feature of the reel that could be set so as to allow line to be stripped back off of it. If the pull of the fish threatened to be greater than the pound test of the line, the drag would give to not break it. Also, the pole was designed so the flexing gave with the surges of the fish fighting against it, thus easing the pull on the line.

Even though Sandy gained a little line with his furious cranking on the handle of the reel, the big fish would strip more back off. This gain-a-little, lose-a-lot of line went on for several minutes until the fish began to tire. That was exactly what the drag and flexing pole were designed for. Gradually, the spool on Sandy's reel began to fill back up.

Sandy was a happy boy. This was the adventure he lived for. Although catching this fish didn't displease him, he didn't like the way this one played. It didn't make runs like it should. It just kind of wove back and forth and struggled against him. He was pretty sure he didn't have a king. Sure enough, when he got the creature near the boat, he could see it was a hammerhead shark. And it was a big one that made his muscles ache while he was reeling it in.

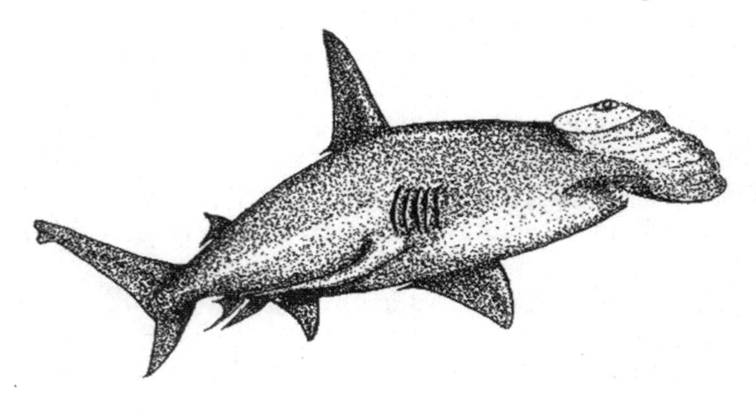

Although shark meat was good to eat, Sandy didn't have room for this five-foot specimen in the boat, and he didn't want to share the space with the vicious teeth or sandpaper skin, either. There was no way he wanted to fool with getting the hook out of its mouth full of teeth, so he reached down the taut leader and cut the hook off with his pliers. He knew that a hook would rust out of the creature's mouth in a matter of days and, thus, not harm it. Sandy did not like to harm wild life. Sandy recited the rule in his head: *The only reason to kill is if you want to eat it or it intends to eat you.*

The monster flipped its large tail and swam away from the boat. Sandy quickly threw the silver trout on his second pole out and allowed it to drift back among the chum on the water in the distance. He inflated more fish and tossed them in with more chum from the bucket and let the sea anchor back out. The chum bucket was really getting a rank aroma now as the sun's rays warmed the dead creatures' bodies. It didn't bother Sandy, however, as the smell of the sea had been part of his existence since birth actually before, because of his parents and their parents before them who were all from the fishing village. He wiped his hands on his shorts again.

He watched his bait and threw in more chum while twisting the wire on the leader to attach another treble hook on the line he had cut off. He prepared another silver trout and hooked it to the line. He rarely took his eyes off of the chum line and his bait, however, and it wasn't long before he had more action in it. This time the splashes were larger and quicker. This was what he was looking for.

Sandy set the second pole down in the boat and pulled in the sea anchor, never taking his eyes off the feeding splashes that came nearer and nearer his bait. The alarm on his reel went off! The fish hit with a furious splash, and the line started stripping off of his reel with the clicker whirring like mad. Sandy grabbed the pole out of the rod holder, turned off the clicker, and set the drag. He was careful to keep the tip of the rod up so it could help fight the fish. If he let it point toward the fish, it would lose the flexibility that helped him keep from breaking the line. This was a nice fish, and it was making a furious run, stripping line off as it went. A king mackerel was an extremely fast-swimming creature. In his mind's eye, Sandy could see the long, slender body that was shaped like a silver torpedo as it raced away.

Sandy had a huge grin on his face as he fought the enormous creature on the other end of his line. This was what living was all about. He was in his element, and he loved it. Finally, after the get line on the reel, lose line back-off-of-it struggle, he started gaining on the creature that was tiring out from the exertion of fighting against the pull of the pole. The youngster's muscles were starting to ache from the exertion. He was fighting a fish that weighed almost half as much as he did. Of course, he had the advantage because of his equipment, but it was still exhausting.

He finally dragged the fish close to the boat and recognized it as a king, but the fish saw the boat, reacted in fear, and took off on another furious run, which stripped the hard gained line back off of the pole. Sandy groaned and grinned. He had expected that, but his arms were aching with the pain of exertion. He kept the pole tip up and continued reeling, even though he wasn't gaining much line.

The king tired, and Sandy began to get her close to the boat. He made another feeble run, and then another, but he had succeeded in tiring her out so much that she rolled on her side when he got her close to the side of *Out Back*. Holding the pole under his left arm and using his right on the gaff, which was a stainless steel, sharpened rod of metal, curved into a "J" shape and attached to a hollow aluminum pole. Sandy hooked him and pulled the silver torpedo over the gunwale and into the boat. Once the king hit the floor it started flopping rapidly. It was at least four and a half or five feet long, and that was a lot of fish. She sounded like the drums in a marching band as it beat against the bottom. Sandy just stayed out of the way and tried to catch his breath and rest his arms. When the fish calmed down, Sandy used his needle-nosed pliers to remove the hook. The fish was too big for his cooler, so he shoved it in the empty ice-stuffed chum bag and that he had brought for the occasion. The big fish still flopped a bit, but the flopping had slowed down. Sandy was elated. This trip was paid for, and a few more would be also with the sale of this big fish.

Sandy tossed the sea anchor back in the water and let the silver trout he had hooked on the other line out. He inflated and tossed more chum in the water. He was pleased that he was going to make his fisherman father proud of his accomplishments this day. Sandy had intentionally avoided telling him where he was fishing and for what, because he wanted to surprise him. There was no doubt he would catch more fish. It was getting close to ten-thirty in the morning, and he still had a couple hours to fish before he needed to head back to the docks.

He didn't see the splashes as before. He was rigging the line he just caught the king on with another bait. The alarm clicker on the reel started to whir; the pole was bent almost double. That was always an extremely exciting sound to him. Sandy grabbed the pole out of the rod holder and set the drag. He held the tip up, holding the pole with his left hand, as he pulled the sea anchor up with his right. It was important to not let the line go slack. If he did, the fish could throw the hook out of its mouth.

This was another big fish. Sandy was beginning to wonder if he had enough strength to catch many more of these. His young body was screaming "You've had enough," from almost every muscle. Regardless, he was a tough youngster, and he would not give up.

He struggled against the big fish, until he finally had it near the boat. It too, had turned on the side, and he gaffed it and hauled it over the gunwale of the boat. It was huge, even larger than the first, and it set up a cacophony of machine-gun beats against the deck as it flopped about. When it slowed down, he used his needle-nosed pliers, removed the hook, and slid it in with the other king fish. Sandy had to be very careful when he removed the hook. It was easy to see that the big king's mouth was full of snow-white, razor sharp teeth. He added more ice to the chum bag and covered them up. It was time for another sandwich and another bottle of water.

Sandy dropped new bait and more chum over the side and threw the sea anchor back in the water. He was very excited about the fish he was catching. It wouldn't take many of these giants to add up to a huge amount of gas money. He had forgotten about the time in his excitement. In the next couple of hours, he caught two more kings and had four boated and iced down in the chum bag. The sun had climbed to directly overhead and started heading for the horizon in the west. Noon had passed.

Sandy was happy about the fish he had in the boat. The thought was distracting him, and he forgot about the time. He decided to try and catch one more before heading for shore. Fishing was just too good. A little sea breeze had picked up and was a comforting respite against the heat of the day. Sandy didn't notice that it had shifted and was now coming from the west. He dumped the last of the chum from the bucket and rinsed it out. He was glad to be rid of the stinking mess. He had just returned the bucket to the floor of the boat when the reel went off again.

This time, however, line continued to be stripped off the reel. Sandy couldn't turn the fish. The line was nearly completely stripped from the reel, so he started the engine, put it in gear, and followed the fish while reeling to get line back on his spool. The big fish was headed east. He would get line back on, and the fish would strip it off, and he followed with the boat to keep from running out of line or breaking it. Thirty minutes later, it seemed as if the fish were beginning to tire.

Sandy was so engrossed in this new monster he had on his line that he failed to notice that one by one, the other boats had turned east and headed for port. He was now the only boat left in the area.

He had probably followed the fish ten or more miles to the east, away from shore, trying to catch it. It was still too much for him to pull in, so he kept the boat going towards the fish. Sandy was exhausted and almost at the end of his ability to fight the monster.

Finally, after what seemed to be an eternity, Sandy saw the fish. *Cobia*! *And it's a big one, probably sixty-five or seventy pounds.* He got a good gaff hook-up near the head and threw his pole into the boat so he could haul on the gaff with both hands. This was a lot of meat and it would mean some serious money.

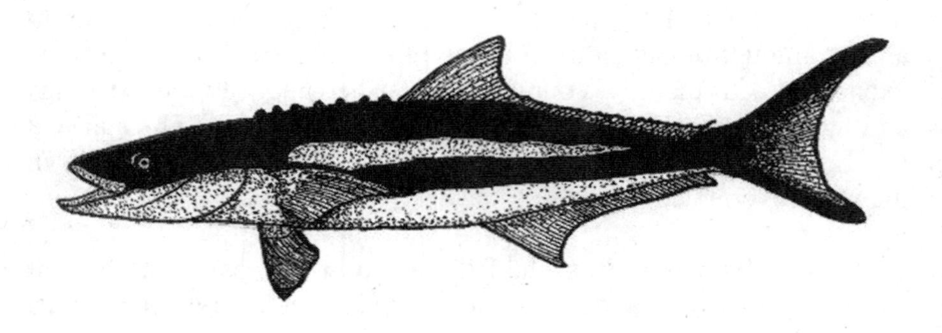

Cobia was a high-dollar fish. It was all he could do to slide the behemoth's head over the gunwale of the boat. Sandy wasn't sure he had enough strength to get a fish that was almost as big as he was in the boat. It was flipping its tail so hard, it was making a white froth out of the water. Then it gave a huge flip, which caused it to shoot up and over the gunwale, and it landed in the bottom of the boat. The gaff flew out of Sandy's hands, and he had to jump out of the way to keep from being crushed.

Sandy stared at the massive, powerful fish. His thick body was almost entirely solid muscle. It hit the floor like an atom bomb and went crazy. It started flipping so hard it was tearing the boat to pieces, but Sandy couldn't do a thing but stay out of the way. The fish could easily break his arm or leg with the mighty pounding it was doing. It flung itself into the air and came down on the center console, tearing it out of the floor. A shower of sparks came from the electric wires as they were snapped in two. The engine stopped, and the battery started smoking. Both caps, where the battery was filled with water, popped off.

Horrified, Sandy was sitting on the bow with both feet up on the gunwales, trying to stay out of the way of the maniacal fish. Now he was in shock as he surveyed the damage to his boat. There was smoke coming from the hole in the floor where the center console had been bolted, so he dipped a bucket of water and poured it into it. Hissing steam blossomed up when the water touched the smoldering mass. The fish had finally stopped flopping and was lying on its side, gill flaps opening and closing. It still gave an occasional feeble flop, but it was done. The creature's roving evil eye followed all of Sandy's movements as if it would strike if given a chance.

Sandy stood up and looked around. There was nothing but water as far as he could see. The flag marking EF was nowhere to be seen. The wind that had shifted out of the west was getting stronger. An ominous, billowing blue-black cloud appeared low over the horizon to the west, and it stretched from horizon to horizon, north and south. Brilliant, jagged, silver strokes of lightning flashed brightly against the darkness of the cloud.

Sandy thought about throwing the anchor over to stop his progress, but he didn't have enough rope for it to reach the bottom, even if it would hold in this storm. He put one of the life jackets on. At three-thirty Saturday afternoon, the first drumbeats of cold rain started pelting his body. This joined the sheets of spray-laden water that were coming over the bow. Fortunately, he kept a hooded rain jacket on board, and he put that on over the life jacket. It was some comfort against the water.

The long rope he used to tie up the boat was lying on the deck. Sandy tied one end around his waist and the other to a cleat on the starboard gunwale. He didn't want to get swept away from the boat. That would finish him off for sure. He knew the boat had positive flotation, which meant that even if it filled with water or capsized, it would still float. His only hope was to stay with the boat. Sandy was really worried. He well knew the wrath of a storm at sea. He was wondering if he was making plans that would save his life.

Sandy sat down on the floor. With his weight in the bottom, it would make the boat more stable. The bilge pump was also dead, so he took the white bucket and began to bail the rapidly accumulating water from the bottom of the boat. His whole body ached, and he had to force himself to keep bailing.

He needed a break, so he reached in the cooler and got another bottle of water and another sandwich. He had been too busy trying to survive to eat his lunch and he was starving. A brilliant flash was immediately punctuated with a deafening boom. A stroke of lightning hit the water ten yards from the boat. His ears went numb from the blast.

If there was anything Sandy hated on the water, it was lightning. It really frightened him. For once, he felt very small and not the least bit in control as he usually did when he was on the water. He was being pushed farther and farther from shore. He guessed he was moving at least five or six knots. The time was after six in the evening and the sky quite dark because of the storm clouds. He was at least forty or forty-five miles from shore now. A sobering thought hit Sandy suddenly. *The stream! The Gulf Stream. It's only about sixty miles from shore here. If I get pushed into that, the current will sweep me northeast towards Europe.*

As a young man, Sandy was struggling against several emotional streams in life: the middle school bullies who had no regard for rules or reason; his immature class peers who constantly degraded him; and the sweet, pretty Gracie who stirred new feelings in his stomach. A new stream--one that was a sudden physical threat to his very life--would teach Sandy that life's lessons are hard, but the process of survival would mold him into a fine man capable of handling any future challenges.

CHAPTER VIII – THE STREAM

Jeanette had her raincoat pulled over her head as she ran up the sidewalk to the house with a bag of groceries under her arm. She leaned over and dropped the bag on a chair and took off the raincoat, which she left on the porch, before she carried the groceries to the kitchen. She had just come from Terry's Country Store in Atlantic Beach where she purchased steaks and vegetables for supper. Terry's was known for its butcher shop and fine meat. She tossed the steaks on the counter and stacked the other groceries in the cabinet. It was six in the evening, and the storm was roaring outside. Jeanette had no idea her young son was lost at sea in the middle of it.

Jeanette removed the steaks from the plastic wrappers, placed them on a cookie sheet and began to spice them up. The front door closed, and Steve walked into the kitchen. "Damn, this is the worst storm we've had in a while. It got real nasty out there. Fortunately, I got in and tied up before it hit. You got steaks. Great! I'm going upstairs to wash up."

The roasting steaks made the kitchen smell heavenly. She prepared mashed potatoes and gravy, Brussels sprouts, green beans, and iced tea. It was another of her men's favorite suppers. Steve came back in the kitchen and sat down at the table. "Jeanette, that smells wonderful. I'm so hungry I could eat a buffalo."

Chad walked in the kitchen. "Hi, Dad. How was fishin'?"

"I did pretty good. You wanna' go get your brother? We're about ready to eat."

"You mean he's not here? He isn't in our room either."

"Sandy's not here? Damn. Jeanette, you might as well put my steak back in the oven to keep it warm. I gotta' go look for the boy. This isn't like him."

A worried look descended over Jeanette's face. But she was a fisherman's wife, and they were used to overcoming adversity. She also knew Sandy was relatively safe in the river and waterways so close to dry land.

Steve pulled on his yellow rain slickers and white rubber boots. As a fisherman, he had the proper foul-weather gear. He had the hood pulled tight against his head, and the cold rain was stinging his face as he walked toward the docks. Sandy's boat wasn't there. He had confidence in his young son's ability on the water and felt something must have happened to the engine or he had run out of gas. Or, maybe, by the time he got to the river from the waterway in the storm, the waves would be too high for him to enter it. If that was the case, the boy would have pulled into shore and taken refuge against the storm.

One thing was for certain, however, it would be futile to try to get a boat on the river in this gale. They would just have to wait it out until morning. He walked back toward the house deep in thought. He was a fisherman and had gone through many things in his life. Sandy would be all right.

Steve went over to the radio when he got back to the house. "This is Stevens base calling the *Out Back*, come in Sandy. Home base calling the *Out Back*, Sandy, are you out there?" No response came back from the radio so Steve placed the microphone back on the receiver.

When he walked back into the kitchen and sat down at the table, Jeanette and Chad looked expectantly at him. "Boat's not there, and he doesn't answer the radio. He probably had engine trouble and pulled up on shore to take refuge against this storm. We'll have to wait until this storm abates before I can go look for him. I'll be right back. I'm going to call the coast guard and the marine patrol and tell them we have a missing person. Did Sandy tell anyone where he intended to fish?"

Both Jeanette and Chad shook their heads. Steve walked to the living room and looked up the numbers. "Yes, I need to report a missing person. It's my son, Sandy Stevens." Steve was answering the guardsman's questions. "He's fourteen, about five-feet-six with close-cropped hair and blue eyes. The boat is a white nineteen-foot fiberglass deep "V" hulled craft with a 100 hp Evinrude engine. I'll have to get back to ya with the hull identification numbers. I need to look them up. He left at daylight and didn't tell us where he intended to fish, but he usually runs up the waterway to the north of the river. Sandy is a very experienced boatman regardless of his age. He doesn't show off or take chances. Yeah, I'm his father, Steve. We live over here on Palmer, and I'm a fisherman. When this storm subsides, I'll start looking for him. Most likely he had engine trouble and pulled up on the bank to take refuge from the storm."

Steve gave the Coast Guard his phone number, hung up, and called the Florida Marine Patrol. Then he returned to the kitchen. "They'll send a boat and a chopper out. I told 'em he usually fishes north on the waterway, so they will look there. I doubt he is fishing in the river. At least we've got some things started. Sandy's got a good head on his shoulders. Everything is going to be alright." Jeanette just shook her head. Mothers always worry.

They stayed up to watch the Ten O'clock News on Channel 12. The weather forecaster had radar pictures of the storm. It was huge, stretching from the Gulf of Mexico, all the way across Florida and out into the Atlantic Ocean. Winds had been gusting up to sixty miles per hour, which were close to hurricane force, and record amounts of rain had fallen. From the radar, it looked as if the storm would last the night and maybe another day.

The news anchor came on with the latest news. Steve and Jeanette were startled by her pronouncement. *"And the latest news is a missing person report. First Coast News has just learned that the son of a Mayport fisherman, Mayport Middle School student Sandy Stevens, has been reported missing."* Sandy's school yearbook picture flashed up on the screen. *"Sandy went fishing this morning and hasn't returned as of this time. It is felt that he developed engine trouble and has probably taken refuge from the storm on a bank of the Intracoastal Waterway. If anyone has any information about Sandy, phone the Coast Guard station in Mayport, Florida. And now for other news . . ."*

Steve clicked the remote and turned the television off. "They listen in on the radio for news and probably heard the Coast Guard talking about this. Actually the publicity might help us if someone has any information. It's going to be a big day tomorrow." He and Jeanette wouldn't be able to sleep much this night.

Gracie's mother walked quietly into her daughter's bedroom and gently shook her shoulder. Gracie moaned a little sigh and opened her eyes. "What's the matter, Momma?"

"Sorry, honey, but I've just seen the ten o'clock news. Isn't your friend's name Sandy Stevens? I thought you'd want to know."

Gracie sat up in bed. Her eyes were suddenly wide-awake and as big around as poker chips. "What's happened, Momma?"

"He didn't return home from fishing today. He's missing. They don't know anything else. The Coast Guard's out looking for him now. The poor boy's caught out there somewhere in this horrible storm. My, my, he seems awfully young to have this much freedom on a boat."

"Oh, no. Momma, that can't be true. We were supposed to go boating tomorrow. It has to be somebody else. Are you sure they said Sandy Stevens?"

"Yes, honey. They even had a picture of him, but I don't know what he looks like. The boy in the picture had real short hair. Nice looking boy."

"Oh, no. It is him. Poor Sandy. What else is going to happen to him? Thanks for telling me, Momma. Yes, I did want to know. I don't know if I can get back to sleep now. We were supposed to go boating tomorrow. Of course we wouldn't be able to in this storm anyway. Please, God, make him all right. He's okay, though. I can feel it."

Gracie's mother pulled the blankets back up around her and kissed her daughter on the forehead. "Good night, sweetheart. I'm sorry your friend is missing, but I'm sure everything will turn out for the best. I think you really like him, don't you? Try to get back to sleep."

"Thank you, Momma. I'm going to say a prayer for Sandy. 'Night, Momma."

Sandy was exhausted. Only sheer guts and determination and a spirit of survival kept him going. He was barely keeping even with the bailing. The fish were sliding all over the deck and crashing into him, so Sandy threw the kings overboard. He tied the big cobia to the stern, however, and it lay there like an evil spirit. One baleful eye seemed to watch him every time a stroke of lightning lit up pitch-black skies and the fish in the boat. It was almost too eerie for Sandy to bear. Suddenly, he felt the air grow warm. *The Stream!*

Sandy had entered the Gulf Stream. It would take him northward at about thirty miles a day. The boat was still tossing like a cork in a washing machine. He was bailing and holding on. The whole floor of the *Out Back* was awash with water. Cold, stinging rain was coming down from above, and warm, frothing waves were coming over the gunwales from below. Sandy was unable to keep up with the bailing. Lightning was crashing down on all sides of the boat. And the malevolent eye of the cobia was keeping watch each time there was a flash of lightning. It was as if the evil fish cast a curse on Sandy, because he had taken its life. Sandy considered throwing the wretched creature overboard, but he might need a meal off of the carcass or maybe use it for bait.

It was five o'clock Sunday morning. Sandy had passed out leaning against the gunwale of the boat a couple hours before. His fatigue was greater than he had ever experienced in his young life. It was more of a condition of somnambulism, as he was somewhere in between sleeping and being awake while he still hung on and tried to keep his balance in the tossing boat. His eyes fought against opening. They were swollen from exposure to so much salt water and the beating he had taken a few days before. His mouth was dry from the salt as well, even though he took occasional swigs of fresh water from one of the bottles.

All of a sudden, Sandy found himself in the water, held afloat by his life jacket. Fortunately, he was still tied to the boat. He was being jerked and towed each time a huge, frothing breaker swarmed over the boat and him. A rogue wave had rolled under the boat and tossed him out. There was another flash of lightning and through stinging eyes, Sandy saw the boat had capsized and was floating upside down.

The waves towered above him like ominous skyscrapers, and then they would crest and break, and a frothing boil of water would come rolling down and engulf him. He struggled to breath and inadvertently swallowed gulps of salt water. It was like being in a strangling watery roller coaster as he was lifted up to the crest of the wave then hurled down the steep side of it to the troth and then was thrust up to the top again.

Although the life preserver kept him mostly on the surface, Sandy was struggling to keep his head above the water that was cascading down over him. The rope tied around his waist was tugging against him as he and the boat were thrust in different directions. His fatigue was enormous, and his whole body ached. He grabbed the rope with his hands. Another giant wave engulfed him, and he was struggling in a swirling mass of bubbles and churning water. *If I don't get out of here soon, I'm a goner. I've gotta get back on the boat.*

Slowly and laboriously, Sandy pulled himself hand over hand back to the boat. He had to hold his breath and put his head down in the water to make headway. Finally he was able to grab one of the handles on the stern of the boat.

Sandy pulled himself over and with every bit of strength he had left, using the foot of the outboard motor as a hand and foot hold, pulled himself up on the bottom of the boat. He lay there exhausted while the waves washed over him. For the first time the thought that he might die crossed his mind. He was very afraid now and didn't quite know what to do. Suddenly, he was merely a fourteen-year-old boy again, but he wouldn't cry.

Finally, a gray tinge lent a little light to the world as dawn came. A huge, light brown fin was slowly circling the boat. Sandy watched, as the shark got bolder and bolder. Finally it came straight for the boat, and Sandy yelled. He pulled his legs and arms in close around his body and watched in fear as the malicious creature swam straight towards where he lay on the bottom of the *Out Back*. But it didn't come after him and dove under the boat instead. He felt the boat jolt and thought that the shark was trying to knock him off into the water. He could see the beast's tail thrashing the water at the side of the boat. Instead, it emerged on the other side with the tail half of the cobia in its mouth.

Much to Sandy's relief, the shark finally swam off content, shaking the cobia to break it apart. That would be a heck of a way to end his life as shark bait. The rain stopped as did the strokes of lightning. The wind also calmed down, and Sandy was glad because he was almost to the end of his strength. He didn't know how much longer he could hold on. The cooler was floating beside the boat, still tied off, but the lid was off and it was empty. Sandy needed a drink, however, his water was tied under the boat. He passed out.

Sandy didn't know how long he had slept, but the sun had come out and the clouds were in the distance. Sandy's tongue felt like somebody had stuck an old shoe in his mouth. He needed water badly. He would have to try to get the fresh water.

Sandy knew he wouldn't be able to get under the boat with the life jacket on, so he took off the raincoat and tied it to the foot of the outboard, which stood up from the stern of the boat, by using the sleeves. Then he took off the life preserver and tied it there as well. Sandy slid down the side of the boat into the water. He was hoping there weren't any more sharks as he took a big breath and dove under the boat.

Oh, my God! He was face to face with the head of the cobia, which was still tied under the boat. The evil eye was watching him again. Sandy had to come back up for air. He took several big breaths, and he dove under once more. He found a jug of water, untied the rope from the boat and surfaced. Painfully, he pulled himself back up on the bottom of the boat and put his life preserver on again. He took a sip of water. Even though he was very thirsty, Sandy knew he must save his water. He tied the jug to the outboard.

Now Sandy was subjected to another extreme. The sun was burning him up. Even though it was hot, he made a shelter over his head with the raincoat. The sea had calmed down, and he drifted with the current, steadily north. The wind had turned southerly, and Sandy was sure that increased the speed at which he was drifting in the stream. A thought passed through his head and he shuddered. *Swiss Family Robinson lasted 37 days lost at sea. That seems like an awfully long time. I don't know if I can make that.*

Steve had dozed off several times during the night, but he mostly sat in his chair and thought. About five that morning, he found Jeannette in the kitchen. "What's the matter? Couldn't you sleep?"

"No, I worried all night. He's my baby. We have to find him."

"We'll find him today. I'm gonna' see what the weather is doing." He walked into the living room and clicked the remote. He switched the TV to the weather channel and was relieved to see the storm was abating faster than expected. It would be clear by noon. That was extremely good news. After trying to raise Sandy on the radio again, Steve walked back into the kitchen to tell Jeannette.

"The news channel says the storm is breaking up faster than expected. That's good, because I'll be able to get out and look for Sandy. Jeannette perked some coffee. "I'm going with you to look for him too. I'll get ready. When do you think we can get out in the boat?"

"Well, I can tell the wind has died down. I'll have to take a look at the river and see how big the waves are. It shouldn't be long. I'm gonna' call the other fishermen. They'll all help."

An unwritten rule in Mayport mandated that fishermen took care of their own. When a person lived by and worked on the ocean, they knew that danger was present every second. If one of them needed help, it was important to get it. Therefore, all fishermen took it seriously when one of their fellows needed help. Everyone literally dropped everything if it was serious enough. Steve started phoning the other families. By noon, there would be dozens of boats looking up and down the river and all over the Intracoastal Waterway.

It was noon and Sandy was starving for food. The contents of the cooler had spilled out, along with the last sandwich. He got the head of the cobia and pulled it up on the bottom of the boat. With his pocketknife, he cut a piece of meat from the back of the remaining part of the cobia. It was snow white meat. *Heck, people eat sushi, this can't be too bad.*

The taste of raw fish wasn't bad, and it served the purpose of sating his hunger. Again, that awful eye watched him as he slowly chewed the meat he had cut from the creature's back. Sandy stared back at the evil eye while he took bites of meat. *You're trying to defeat me, you awful devil. But it won't work. I won't let you beat me.* He stowed the head with his gear by the foot of the outboard motor. The weight of the engine made the boat sink slightly at the stern, which made the bottom of the boat slant upwards toward the bow. Sandy's small size and weight were assets to him because the nineteen-foot hull of the *Out Back* was relatively large by comparison.

Another shark had taken up residence and circled the boat ominously. Sandy didn't know if it smelled the cobia or what the attraction was, but he didn't like the company. He climbed higher toward the bow of the boat. He wished he had a weapon. In what seemed like no time at all, another night fell upon him.

Floating on the ocean, lying stomach down on the bottom of the upturned boat, Sandy rested his chin on his arms and looked down into the sea. It was alive with a kaleidoscope of color as a myriad of different sea life zoomed back and forth, leaving their phosphorescent trails behind. It was like looking down from a helicopter at a busy freeway after dark. His stomach sounded like a dogfight as it churned for lack of food, and his mind was like a beehive, abuzz with thoughts of his predicament. Sandy knew he would have to solve this food dilemma if he was to survive and he was running out of water rapidly, even though he was trying to conserve it. Finally, he drifted off into a fit-full sleep.

The flotilla of fishermen left the docks as soon as the water in the river calmed enough. Steve's friend and fellow fisherman Rick Hoffman made up a search plan and gave each boat captain a certain place on the river or Intracoastal to search so the boats would be spread out. Steve and Jeanette would wander to the different locations Steve had shown Sandy. They also went to those places Sandy had told him he fished. It was eleven in the morning.

By five that evening, the boats had all returned to the docks and tied up. All of the fishermen met at Mr. Roland's fish house. No one had seen anything. Since it was Sunday, the workers weren't present. Mr. Johnny Bryant was driving past the fish house and happened to see the crowd of local fishermen. He stopped to see what was happening. He walked up to Matt Roland. Matt was a kindly gentlemen and much loved in Mayport. He was tall and thin and partially balding and renowned for his charity among the people. He was a very intelligent man and an avid reader. "Hi, Mr. Roland. What's all the commotion about?"

"We've been searching for Sandy Stevens. He didn't return from fishing yesterday, and Steve thought that he might have had engine trouble and pulled the boat up on a bank in the waterway or river. Everybody has searched since noon, but there was not a trace of him. This is pretty serious."

"Wait a minute. You been searchin' the river 'n the waterway for Sandy? He didn't go fishin' in the river. When he got ice, he told me he was goin' after king fish and he would chum for 'em. I tole him to be careful 'bout the weather and he said he knew. I was busy down at the fish house until late last night because of the storm. I didn't hear the news."

Mr. Roland was staring at Johnny Bryant, digesting what he had just heard. "Come with me!"

He led Johnny over to where Steve stood talking to a group of fishermen. "Steve, I think you need to hear what Johnny has to say. Tell him Johnny." Johnny related what he had just told Mr. Roland to Steve and the other fishermen. The look on Steve's face darkened as he heard what was being said.

"Damn! I gotta' get fueled up. I'm goin' out. Matt, will you call the Coast Guard and tell them? Chum fishin' he said?" Johnny nodded yes. "That means he got chum from a shrimp boat—probably the *Miss Corrine.* I need to talk to Al. Can I use your phone, Matt?"

Mr. Roland nodded, and Steve hurried into the office. One of the other fishermen told Jeanette the news. She lifted a clenched fist to her mouth and a tear started coursing down her cheek. Sandy had been gone two days and a night by now, and the sun had slipped beneath the horizon.

Steve had Cap'n Alpo on the phone. "Hey, Al, I don't know if you've heard, but my son Sandy is missing. I was wonderin' if he got chum from ya' and if he mentioned where he would fish?"

"Damn, Steve, I'm sorry to hear that. No, I hadn't heard about it. Buddy and I were down at the dock makin' sure Miss Corinne weathered the storm until late. I came home in the early mornin' and just fell in the bed. I'm gonna' be at the dock in an hour to help ya' search. Sandy did get chum from us, but Buddy Mims talked to him. I was at the helm during the time. I can give ya' Buddy's number."

"Yeah, Al, give it to me. I need to call him. And thanks for the offer to help." Steve dialed Buddy's number. "Hello."

"Buddy, this is Steve Stevens."

"Hey Steve, how ya' doin?"

"Actually, I've been better. Sandy never came home yesterday and has been missing two days and a night now. I heard he got chum from ya'. Did he say where he intended to fish?"

"God, Steve, that's awful. I told him to watch out for that storm and leave for home early. He told me he knew about the storm and would leave for the docks by twelve. Yeah, we talked, yelled actually. He said he was goin' to try *Nine Mile*. I told him that the reports I had about fish were a little farther out at *EF,* and he said he'd try that. I'm pretty sure that's where he went."

"Thanks, Buddy."

"Steve, did Cap'n Alpo say he was goin' out to help search?"

"Yeah, Buddy, he did."

"I'll be at the dock in ten minutes. I'm goin' with him. I'm sorry about your son, but don't worry, we'll find 'em. Sandy's a smart and able boy."

"Thanks, Buddy. I appreciate that. I'll see ya'. Got lots to do."

Steve's boat was a forty foot snapper boat which had an enclosed cabin including sleeping space. Both Chad and Jeanette told him they were going along. They would be able to spend several days out on the ocean if necessary, and Jeanette started throwing provisions into paper bags. The Coast Guard dispatched a cutter and a helicopter immediately. Al Butler called all the shrimpers he knew, and an unbelievable number of different types of boats would be headed out towards *Nine Mile* and *EF*.

Although his conversation with the Coast Guard confirmed what he already knew, Steve discussed the weather, and especially the gale force westerly winds, with the other fishermen. If Sandy had engine trouble—and most certainly that was what had happened—he would have been blown seriously east and could have ended up in the Stream. There was the possibility, however, he was able to get an anchor down and could still be in the *EF* area. But, that was highly unlikely. Steve knew Sandy fished almost exclusively inland and wouldn't have the one-hundred fifty feet of line necessary to successfully anchor up in that deep water, even if it would have held in the storm.

Most of the boats provisioned up. In addition to fuel, they had enough ice and food to last several days. Now Steve was worried. Everything had changed. Looking for a tiny nineteen-foot boat in the broad expanse of the Atlantic Ocean was like looking for a grain of salt in a gravel road. And, if Sandy had reached the Stream, he was headed north, and that complicated things even more. It was comforting to Steve to know that his brothers were concerned for his progeny and were out in force to help. In times like these, the more searchers helping, the more likely Sandy would be found.

Steve also realized he hadn't felt that all-pervading sense of doom. He was psychically connected to his son who was so much like him, and he was sure that if Sandy had died, he would have felt it. Steve knew Sandy was still alive. He had to hurry, though. It had already been too long. Food and water—especially water, were huge issues. The dangerous sea life, like sharks, could be a problem too.

The day was getting dark again. Sandy had cut several more strips of meat from the awful looking cobia, which continued to stare at him albeit now from a spoiled, clouded eye. He knew the fish was getting too rank to eat. The persistent shark still circled the boat. It seemed to be getting bolder and bolder. It knew fresh meat was on top.

Sandy kept watching the wicked fin that cut through the water on the surface of the ocean. Fear surged through his body when it turned, cut the water straight toward the boat, and a huge face and jaw crunched down on the side of the boat and shook it violently. *Oh God, it's a Great White.* Sandy held on for dear life. He had discovered a line floating on the other side of the boat from the one which was tied to his waist and pulled it up and tied it to the other side of his body. This helped secure him in the middle of the bottom of the *Out Back.* He could see the beast's devil eye move back and forth as it evaluated him like a hobo looking through a Burger King window at a Whopper. Sandy didn't like it, and he was terrified.

The shark was almost as large as the boat. He grabbed the remains of the cobia, which was still two or three feet long, untied it, and hurled it overboard.

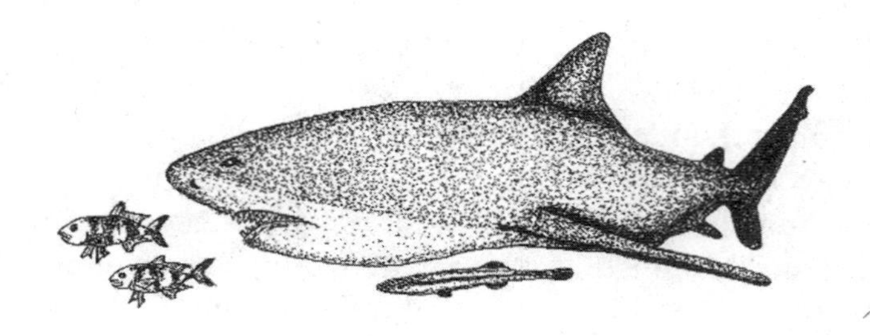

It worked. The shark disappeared, chasing the cobia head. It may have thought it succeeded in dislodging the inhabitant on top of the boat, because it didn't return. Sandy didn't have any more food, and he would have to dive under the boat again to get more fresh drinking water that was he tied there before the storm hit. It was really scary to him to get into the water after the shark encounters he had. At least he had water. Many of the things Sandy had done, were now saving his life. It was dark again. At least tied off as he was, he could try to sleep. Actually, as tired as he was, he passed out and didn't awaken until daylight.

The men decided that nothing could be done until daybreak. It would be impossible to search in the dark. The search team would set out in the wee hours of the morning, so they could arrive at the area to be searched just as the sun came up. At two in the morning, the flotilla of boats was out in the dark heading for the vicinity of *EF*. Others would head straight northeast to the stream. Some of the faster boats wouldn't leave until later. Again, Rick Hoffman had devised a search plan and distributed it to the captains. Steve, Cap'n Alpo and several others were headed northeast for the stream north of the area. The Coast Guard had done a calculation using wind speed, current, and water speed to try and approximate where Sandy could be. Steve and Cap'n Alpo were using those coordinates.

Unfortunately, the calculations were made from *EF*. They couldn't know that Sandy chased the fish for several miles further east and that the calculations would be off by quite a bit. Sandy was a lot farther away than was predicted. Jeanette sat in the seat next to the helm and searched the sea with desperate eyes. The snapper boat was not a fast boat, and it would be three or four hours before it got to the area they wanted to search. Once they got close, they would zig zag back and forth across the stream in a search pattern.

Sandy slept like he was dead. He was totally exhausted. That night he was visited by Gracie. He was dressed like Rhet Butler in Gone With the Wind. Gracie was dressed like Scarlett O'Hara. They were waltzing in front of a huge crowd. In his dream, Sandy was a head taller than Gracie, and she had her hair done so that her blond curls fell in golden cascades past her shoulders. That strange, unidentified feeling when he was around her, overcame him again. When he awoke, it was sometime Monday morning. He was almost irritated that the sun had interrupted his dream. He was still in a daze that the dream had created. By the height of the sun, he reasoned it must be eight thirty or nine. It took a few minutes for his head to clear and remember where he was. Before his dream of Gracie, he had a horrible nightmare that a school of sharks had attacked him and bit off his arms and legs.

Sandy had to rinse out his eyes with some of the fresh water to get them completely open. They were swollen and loaded with crust. The sun had also taken its toll on his face and arms. Even though he tried to stay covered with the raincoat, the relentless sun reflected off every wave. The wind had picked up again, and the sea was choppy. The sun was out, however, and visibility was good.

Although Sandy kept the ropes tied to his body, he loosened them so he could stand up and relieve his cramped legs. He surveyed his world. Water was everywhere as far as his eyes could see. Sandy was wondering if he would ever be picked up. He was famished. He thought of his fishing poles tied to the gunwale beneath the boat. He still had a piece of cobia in his pocket that was too rancid to eat, but maybe it could be used for bait. He took off the life preserver again and carefully tied it to the foot of the outboard.

After looking carefully around to be sure no shark fins were around, he slipped over the side. Taking a huge breath, he dove down and untied one of the poles. He still had the rope attached to his waist. Sandy surfaced holding the pole, and his blood froze. Twenty yards away, a huge brown fin was cutting the water coming in his direction. He flung the pole up on the bottom of the boat and hauled himself out of the water and scrambled up on the bottom of the boat just as a ten-foot long monster dove under it.

Sandy's heart was about to pound out of his chest. The shark circled the boat. Sandy put the life preserver back on and scrambled up to the center of the hull. He was relieved when the creature lost interest and swam off in the distance. This would be his last dive under the boat. He was down to his last bottle of water, and he wasn't going to risk being eaten another time. He had left the rope tied to the pole, so he tied it off to the foot of the outboard motor. The boat was slowly bobbing up and down in the water with the wave action.

Sandy was standing up reattaching the second rope when he spotted something in the distance. A black dot appeared on the horizon. He kept his eyes locked on the dot. It would disappear then reappear as the boat floated to the crest of a swell and then floated down the troth. Then it grew larger. It was a vessel of some kind. Sandy began to get excited. He would be rescued. Seconds stretched into minutes and he watched the boat. Fifteen minutes later, he could see it was a large freighter steaming south.

He began to wave his bright yellow raincoat. The freighter was moving by two miles west of where Sandy was. He kept waving the raincoat. He had to get the attention of whoever was on the bridge. Now the freighter was even with his position, only it was still over two miles away. But the little boy was only a speck in the huge expanse of ocean, and the helmsman was used to dozens of crossings and hours on end without seeing any other signs of human life. Then the freighter was past him, and Sandy watched, holding the raincoat down at his side dejectedly, as the huge craft got smaller and smaller and smaller in the distance. This time Sandy cried. He didn't bawl or sob, but tears of pent-up frustration, disappointment, weariness, and anxiety streamed down his face.

Gloomily, he tied the raincoat to the outboard and picked up the fishing pole. Using his knife, he cut off three pieces of the spoiled meat and put one on each of the three prongs of the treble hook. He wished he had a better hook but at least he had this one. He slid the corks all together at the swivel where the line was attached to the leader. That done, he sat down and tossed the bait in the water.

Things that floated in the water always attracted little fish. It was the case with the *Out Back.* The bait attracted immediate activity. Soon there was a boil of fish bodies around the bait. Sandy jerked on the pole and reeled in. He had a little fish on the hook. It hadn't been caught by the mouth, however. When he jerked on the pole, the fish was impaled through the side with one of the hook's three prongs. It didn't matter to Sandy how he caught it, he had a fish. It was about eight inches long. He unhooked it and stuck it in his pocket.

Soon he had four little fish in his pocket. When he caught the fifth, he hooked it through the tail and tossed it back in. Now he would see if he could catch a larger one. He tied the pole tightly to the foot of the outboard and got out a fish and his pocket knife. The knife was starting to rust from exposure to salt water.

Sandy cut the little strips of meat from the sides of each fish and skinned it. He popped the raw fish into his mouth. Contrary to the cobia, these tasted awful. Still, he needed the nutrition if he was to keep up his strength and he got another one out of his pocket. Sandy was making horrible faces and struggling not to gag so he could swallow the meat. Although there wasn't much food from the four little fish, it was enough for now. The clicker on the reel went off, and Sandy's head jerked up in time to see a large, brown fin and the tip of a slowly undulating tail moving away from the boat. The shark had taken the little fish and was swimming off with Sandy's hook in its mouth. It stripped every bit of Sandy's line from the reel, broke it off from the pole, and disappeared into the distance. The pole was now useless, but he wasn't going back under the boat for the other one unless he was forced to. He didn't have any more bait, anyway.

Something sounded like a jet airliner was taking off. Sandy had fallen asleep shortly after noon. The noise got closer and closer, and Sandy awoke with a start and sat quickly up on the bottom of the boat. Then his astonished eyes popped open wide like dinner plates. Headed directly for him was the foulest looking waterspout he had ever seen. It was black and furious. The ocean was frothing white as the monster sucked up the water from the ocean. The youngster was frozen with fear. There was absolutely nothing he could do. *My God! I will get sucked right off of this boat. I've got to think of something!*

The outward fringes of wind were just starting to suck at him. Sandy hated to do it but he had no choice. He dove off the bottom of the boat and emerged beneath it. The water was swirling furiously and was whipped into frothing bubbles.

Sandy could feel the boat as it was being sucked upwards. He was terrified, and the noise was deafening. Salt water was blown into his face as if it came from a fire hose. He was afraid he was going to be sucked up into the heavens. Then, just as suddenly as it had been lifted, the boat slammed back down onto the sea and covered him once again.

Fortunately, Sandy's luck was still holding. As the behemoth passed about thirty yards just south of his position, it spared him a direct hit.

As soon as he thought it was safe, he swam out from under the boat and climbed back up on it. The waterspout was moving rapidly off in the distance. The little boy could only shake his head at what had just occurred.

Steve's snapper boat was named *Miss Jeanette*. Many fishermen named their boats after their wives and Steve had as well. The *Miss Jeanette* arrived at the search area just as the sun rose. Chad climbed up on the roof. The higher up one was, the better he was able to see far away across the sea. Jeanette had the binoculars and was out on the deck scanning the water with them. Steve was guiding the boat east northeast for ten miles and then he would turn and run west northwest for ten more miles. Sandy was forty miles farther north. Cap'n Alpo was twenty miles south of them doing the same search pattern. The day wore on.

Jeanette ran into the cabin. "Steve, over there." She was pointing out the front window of the cabin to the north east. Steve could make out an object floating on the water and steered for it. As the *Miss Jeanette* pulled up along side the object, Steve put her in neutral and Chad fished the object out of the water with the boat hook. It was a life preserver. Printed across the side were the words *Out Back.*

Steve could see tears well up in Jeanette's eyes. He pulled her to him and hugged her. "Jeanette, this doesn't mean anything except for the fact we are on the right track. Sandy had four life preservers on board, and this is only one of them. He'll have one of them on, I can assure you. He is smart about that. This means he's up north of us somewhere. We have to be getting closer, and we are on the right track. I'll call the Coast Guard on the radio and tell them what we found. Come on now, and let's get back to our search."

She nodded weakly and picked the up binoculars again. Steve put the boat in gear and started his search once more. The day wore on, but they didn't see a trace of Sandy or his boat. It was getting harder and harder for Jeanette. She fixed breakfast on the boat, sandwiches for lunch, and it was getting close to dark, so she would make more sandwiches for supper. Steve would let the boat drift in the stream that night and resume the search in the morning. He and Chad took turns standing watch. It wouldn't do for them to get run down by a freighter.

Another day had passed. The pale yellow sun was about to sink behind the sea in the west. Just then, Sandy spotted an airplane flying low over the water three or four miles east of his position. He could see the tell tale orange color that designated it as a Coast Guard plane. Could they be searching for him? He was sure of it. Mr. Johnny Bryant or maybe Buddy must have finally told them where he went. His hopes started to build again, but slowly sank as the plane disappeared in the distance and the darkness of nightfall started taking over the world.

He must be dreaming again. The rumbling got louder and louder. *The freight train's getting nearer. I have to get off of the tracks.* Sandy was writhing in his sleep, trying to get out of the way of the train. Then his eyes popped open.

In his sleep-drugged state; he wasn't sure whether he was still having the nightmare or not. Suddenly, he was fully awake and he realized the rumbling was real. He looked up from where he lay on the hull of the boat and couldn't believe his eyes. A mammoth ship was bearing down upon him from the north. It was one hundred yards away. The rumbling was the noise of the huge diesel engines that propelled it. The reverberating sound of the huge diesel engines in the still of the darkness was unmistakable. All visages of sleep left his body instantly.

He quickly untied one of the ropes that held him to the bottom and stood up. He didn't know what to do. He could barely see the helmsman in the dimly lit wheelhouse high above the water. In the dark, there was no way he could be spotted. Sandy started to yell and wave, but the ship came on. He could hear the noise of the foam at the bow as the big ship plowed through the water. There were sparks of phosphorescence glowing in the spray. He didn't know if he should jump from the boat and try to swim away from the oncoming, massive ship or to take his chances and wait. He watched in horror as the giant ghost shape bore down on him, and the throb of the engines got louder and louder. In his indecision, he did nothing. The behemoth loomed larger and larger in the darkness of the night. This time, the boy thought his time on earth was over.

Sandy was relieved when the ship passed by on the side of his boat. It was an extremely close call. It passed by so close he could almost touch it. He was dwarfed by the size of the ship.

The huge bow wave lifted the *Out Back* out of the water and turned it over, dumping most of the water out of it in the process. Sandy was flung like a helpless toy on a string into the water, fortunately, still tied to the boat. Sandy hit the water like he had done a belly flop from a high dive diving board. The air was driven from his lungs. Although his life preserver kept him afloat, Sandy was struggling to keep his head above water in the bow waves of the freighter and still get breaths. He was gasping for air, and struggling against the constricted feeling in his chest from having the air knocked out of him. Sandy had heard that a person's whole life passed in front of him at times like these. Not so for Sandy. He wanted to be out of the damned water again, the water that had been so threatening to him so much in the past days. His survival instincts were another aspect that continued to save his life. He was, however, ending up back in the ocean way too much for his liking.

It seemed like forever that the ship steamed past as Sandy swam to the stern of the *Out Back* and used the foot of the outboard to climb aboard. The thud of the enormous diesel engines was very loud now. He couldn't believe what had just happened. He was elated to be able to be in the boat, however, and not clinging to the bottom. There was an empty hole in the floor where the center console had been, and he could see down into the blackened bilge. Sandy got the bucket, which was still tied to the boat and bailed the most of the remaining water out of the boat.

He had lost the last of his fresh water, however, which bothered him. He lay down on the deck and went back to sleep. He was more comfortable on the inside of the boat than he had been in several days roped to the bottom of the hull.

Chad saw the lights of a ship in the distance. He had no idea this very same ship had almost run over his little brother. It would pass harmlessly to the west of them, so he wouldn't have to start the boat and move out of the way. Chad watched the ship as it steamed past and disappeared in the distance to the south. Chad thought of his brother. *Where is he? What is he going through at this moment? Is he still alive? Maybe he's on that freighter or maybe it just passed him by.*

CHAPTER IX – THE RESOLUTION

Sandy awakened much more refreshed the next morning. He searched the boat to see what was left and found a small bottle of water jammed under the starboard gunwale. He sipped a little bit, just enough to wet his mouth good and stowed the bottle in the shade. His raincoat, which was his only protection from the sun, was still tied to the foot of the outboard, so he tipped it up and retrieved the coat. Although the water pacified his thirst, at least partially—his aching stomach was aching for food.

Sandy heard the sound before he spotted where it came from. A Coast Guard helicopter was traveling north about two or three miles east of his position. He stood up and waved the bright yellow raincoat as hard as he could but the copter kept traveling north. Now Sandy was certain they were looking for him. He was too far from land for this to be a coincidence. He was sure he would be spotted soon. He was burned up by the sun, and exhausted, but he was still in pretty good shape. This was mostly due to the water with which he had the foresight to stock his boat. He had a thought and started giggling. *Oh well, I always wanted to see what England looked like.*

This was his fourth day on the water and he had been through a lot. Sandy would never be the same. He had aged years beyond his fourteen on earth from this ordeal of *boy against the sea.* His stomach was growling again. He untied the other pole and dropped the treble hook in the water. He didn't have any bait, but maybe he could snatch-hook a fish. Sandy needed to eat.

Steve, Jeanette, and Chad were up at daylight and resumed their zigzag search pattern. They were still twenty miles from his position. Jeanette was miserable with worry. She searched and searched, desperate to find her son. Steve steered mutely. He was very concerned as well, but he had hope, and he did not have a bad feeling like he would have if Sandy had been struggling against death. It was approaching noon.

Try as he might, Sandy couldn't hook a fish. He heard an engine again. It was the helicopter, and this time it was coming right at him from the south. He threw the pole down and grabbed the bright yellow raincoat and began to wave it wildly and jump up and down. He didn't realize he was hollering, "Here I am. Here I am." The men in the chopper spotted him, and soon it was hovering right above the *Out Back*. Sandy had to shield his eyes from the furious prop wash that was churning up the seas around his boat. A rescue swimmer in a black wet suit dropped out of the chopper. He swam over to the boat and boosted himself over the gunwale into it. He spit out the snorkel and raised his mask. The men in the chopper were lowering a sling at the same time. He had to yell to be heard over the noise of the chopper.

"You Sandy?"

"Yes. Thank God you spotted me this time. You've gone by several times and didn't see me."

"Here, let me get you into this sling."

He slid the sling over Sandy, and the men in the chopper hoisted him up. The rescue swimmer stayed in the boat and rigged a charge to blow it up. It would be dangerous to let it stay afloat in the shipping channel. The sling was lowered back down, and the rescue swimmer was hoisted back aboard the chopper.

Sandy was given a headset to wear since the chopper was too noisy to communicate in without it. The guardsman who had hoisted Sandy up was talking to him. "Are you okay, Sandy? I can see you're burned up, and you have a couple black eyes, but you look pretty good for having spent four days lost at sea."

"I need food and water bad, but I'm fine. I already had the black eyes."

The men handed him a bottle of water and a couple of snack bars. "This is all we have for now, but we'll be back at base soon, and we'll fix you up with a real meal. There are some folks who are going to be mighty happy to hear we found you."

"Thanks, sir. Don't worry about the snack bars bein' all ya' have. Right now an old shoe would taste like a steak, and the water's just what I needed."

The UHF radio on *Miss Jeanette* blurted out raucously. "Calling the Miss Jeanette. This is the United States Coast Guard calling the Miss Jeanette."

Steve grabbed the microphone from the hanger. "United States Coast Guard, you have the Miss Jeanette, go ahead."

"Folks, guess who we have on board with us. We have your son. We found Sandy, and he is fine. We will be in Mayport when you get home."

Not only did cheers emit from the three people on *Miss Jeanette*, they reverberated from boats all over the area as the skippers and crew listened in on the conversation. Steve wheeled the boat around and headed southwest at full speed. He selected his waypoint for the jetties on his GPS and put the boat on autopilot. Jeanette lay down on the couch and passed out from fatigue. She hadn't slept in four days.

Sandy also passed out aboard the helicopter. The events and ordeals that had happened to him and the relief of being rescued left him exhausted. Actually, he had never ridden in a helicopter and intended to enjoy the ride, but it had landed at the Mayport Coast Guard Station when they woke him up. It would be four hours before his family arrived back in Mayport.

The Channel Twelve news crew was waiting at the Coast Guard Station when Sandy got out of the chopper. They interviewed him and recorded some footage on a tape of the interview. Sandy was very shy and mostly answered "yes maam" or "no maam." The crew of the helicopter then escorted Sandy into the Station and gave him a couple of roast beef sandwiches and more water. He couldn't get enough water.

Sandy had to tell the Coast Guard all that had happened for their records. They listened intently, shaking their heads at times that this fourteen-year-old boy was able to do the things he had done and the odds he had overcome. Many full grown men had died at sea during similar circumstances. Finally, they allowed him to leave the station. He lived nearby, so he just walked out.

Sandy went home and took a warm shower. He put on some fresh clothing and walked down to Mr. Roland's Fish House. Mr. Johnny Bryant was still there. He ran over and grabbed Sandy's hand. "Sandy, you're okay. Man I was worried about you. I'm glad you told me where you were going to fish. Made some mistakes, didn't you, son?"

"Yeah, a bunch of them, and I paid for 'em, too. I lost my boat, my rods, my tackle. I lost everything. I'll tell you what. I'm a changed person now."

"But at least you're alive. That's the important thing. Tell me what happened."

Sandy began the long story of the events that occurred the past four days. Johnny listened intently, shaking his head occasionally at some of the things Sandy had gone through. Actually, it was an amazing story.

The double doors of Mr. Roland's fish house that led out to the dock were open. Just as Sandy was finishing his story, the *Miss Jeanette* idled by on the way to moorage. "Mr. Johnny, there goes my family. I'm gonna' walk out on the dock to meet 'em." Sandy trotted out of the door to Mr. Roland's fish house and down the street to the dock. It was a couple of blocks away, but he still got there before the *Miss Jeanette* arrived. He was standing on the dock when Steve guided her through the opening in the docks and brought her up to where Sandy stood.

Chad was standing on the bow and the boys grinned at each other. Sandy tossed him a mooring line then walked down and threw his mother a stern line. Steve cut off the engines as Jeanette leaped from the gunwale onto the dock and literally smothered her young son in her arms. She had tears in her eyes, and she kissed him repeatedly. "Oh, Sandy. Are you all right? You had me so frightened. I never thought I'd see you again. Oh, Honey, you can't ever give me a scare like this again. I don't think I could live through another one."

Steve climbed up on the dock and shook Sandy's hand. "You okay, boy?" Of course, Steve had been very concerned for his young son. But secretly, now that the ordeal was over, he was glad things had happened as they did. The lessons at sea were harsh, and any of them people survived were ones they would never forget. They wouldn't ever make the same mistakes again.

Sandy had just gone through a rite of passage that boosted him far ahead of other boys his age. And, he would never be the same again. All of the *streams* in Sandy's life had suddenly come to resolution.

Steve also knew that Sandy had been punished enough by the trials of the last four days and three nights. He didn't have to add to it by being critical. Characteristically, he didn't say much at all.

"Yes, Dad. I'm fine. I'm pretty tired though. I'll tell you what happened when we get to the house. I did some stupid things you've always warned me about when a person is on the water. Of course, I did some smart things you taught me, too. And those things saved my life. The most important were having plenty of water and a life preserver."

"Let me get this boat tied up and locked down. I'll meet you up at the house." Steve and Chad went about the tasks to secure the *Miss Jeanette*. Jeanette kept her arm around her young son's shoulders as they walked to the house

.

That evening Steve, Chad and Sandy sat at the kitchen table while Jeanette prepared supper. Sandy was telling his story.

"Well, the first thing stupid I did was to not tell you where I was gonna fish. I should have known better, but I wanted to surprise you with a big catch. The second was that maybe I should have put this trip off with the weather predicted to be so bad. But, I only get two days a week to fish, and I could only think about getting' out there.

"Boy, were the fish bitin'. I had strike after strike. The first hook up was a big hammerhead shark. I cut him off and let the bait on my other pole back and hooked up with a nice king. During the mornin', I caught four kings in the thirty to forty pound class. That was a lot of meat, and I was getting' lots of gas money.

"Then came my next big mistake. It was gettin' late, already after twelve, and I got greedy. I was catchin' them so fast, I thought I'd catch one more. This time, though, I hooked into a true monster, the biggest fish I ever hooked up in my entire life. It was strippin' all the line off my pole and headin' east, so I had to crank up and chase it. I was dumb to forget about the time. That put me even farther from shore, probably at least ten more miles."

Steve had an interjection. "So you were farther out than *EF*. Probably thirty to thirty-five miles off shore or more. That explains why we were so far off in our search."

"Yeah, I got so excited about the fish, I forgot everything else, including the time and weather. Finally, I got the fish to the boat. It was the biggest cobia I've ever seen. It was a true monster. All I could think about was all the gas money I was going to make off of this monster, and how proud you'd be of me. I got the gaff in it and threw my pole in the boat. It was so heavy, I didn't think I'd be able to get it in the boat. I had its head over the gunwale when it thrashed its tail and jumped in the boat. Dad, you have never seen anything like that crazed fish. It went nuts!"

"Yeah, them big cobia will tear your boat apart. It's happened to many fishermen before."

"Well, that's exactly what happened to me. I was helpless. All I could do was sit up on the bow with my feet up on the gunwales so it wouldn't break my arm or leg. That monster weighed almost as much as I do. It knocked the center console off the floor and ripped all the wires out. The wires started smoking, the battery blew up, and I had to pour water on the fire. That pretty much cooked my electrical system.

"When I looked up, I knew I was gonna' pay for my stupidity. A storm from the devil was headed my way, and I could do nothing about it. Then I started using my head. I tied everything down, including myself, and especially the water. I put on a life preserver and a raincoat, and I sat as low as possible on the floor. I tried to bail, but I couldn't keep up with the rain coming down and the waves coming over the top of the boat.

"I don't know if I've ever seen it blow so hard, and straight out of the west, too. I knew then that I'd probably end up at the stream, and for the first time, I started worrying about not makin' it. The waves cooked up to twelve to eighteen. I threw the kings overboard. They were dangerous sliding around on the floor and they kept hitting me. Those guys have sharp fins and pointed noses. They were beatin' me up. I kept the cobia, though and tied him off on the stern. I thought I would probably need the meat, either to eat or as bait. It was like an evil creature watching me with that awful eye. I thought it was casting a curse on me, and I thought about throwin' it overboard.

"Then a rogue wave hit, threw me out of the boat and flipped it over. I just about drowned in the awful seas. I couldn't get a good breath. I must have swallowed a gallon of seawater. I knew I had to get out of the ocean. I struggled as hard as I could to pull myself to the boat with the line I had tied around my waist. Dang, am I glad I tied myself off. Finally, I got a hold on the boat and climbed out on to the bottom and roped myself down as best I could." Steve was pleased with the sober thinking his young son had demonstrated as Sandy related the events of the past few harrowing days.

Steve was engrossed in his son's story. When Sandy got to his last statement, he was moved to a few of his rare words. "Son, I love you, and I am glad you made it through this. I don't want ya' to think you are the only fisherman who has had a lesson from the "School of Hard Knocks." Some day, I'll tell you a few of my lessons. Hell, I can tell you stories of dozens of our fellow fishermen from here in Mayport that are just like yours. The important thing is that ya' learn from your mistakes and from ya' words, and it sounds as if ya' have. That's important. If ya' want to be found when there has been an accident, people have to know where to look. I think ya' know that now. Ya' did good, boy. Ya' made some mistakes, but you used ya' head and worked ya' way outa' them. You'll be a fine fisherman." With that, Steve fell silent and took another bite of food.

The television was on in the living room, and the sound drifted in to the kitchen. It was Donna Hicken. *And finally, we have a story with a happy ending. Right after the commercial break, join us to hear the story of a young Mayport Middle School student who was rescued after four days and three nights lost at sea.*

Everyone jumped up and ran for the living room. After the commercial, Donna came back on.

A lot of news doesn't have a happy ending, but tonight we have one that does. We reported last Saturday night that a young

Mayport Middle School student, Sandy Stevens, was missing. He had been out fishing and never returned. After an extensive search, the United States Coast Guard found him alive today in the Gulf Stream. Formerly, it was believed that he was fishing in the St. Johns River or in the waterway. That was incorrect. Sandy had gone fishing in the Atlantic Ocean. Here is footage we shot just hours ago.

The picture changed to the interview of Sandy at the Coast Guard Station. Of course he didn't say much, and the interviewer did almost all the talking with questions.

It cut back to Donna Hicken again. *Among other things, Sandy had a huge cobia wreck his boat and destroy the electrical system, so he couldn't use the radio or start his engine. He got caught in that horrible gale on Saturday and was blown out to the Gulf Stream. A rogue wave capsized his boat and threw him into the water. Sandy showed quite a bit of wisdom for a fourteen-year-old boy, because he had tied himself to the boat. Otherwise he could have been swept away. Using all of his strength, Sandy pulled himself back to the boat, and he spent the rest of the night and the next two days on the upturned bottom of his boat. Sandy had several close encounters with sharks, he had to eat raw fish, dodged a waterspout, and he was almost run over by a giant Freighter. This young man really has a story to tell.*

Donna turned to her co-anchor. "And he's only fourteen years old. Isn't that an unbelievable story? At least this is one story that had a happy ending. You know, I met Sandy today and talked to him. For a fourteen-year-old boy, this young man is amazing. Just talking to him makes you see why he is such a survivor. And, he is so humble."

Sandy was sat grinning sheepishly. "Yeah, and he was one utterly stupid fourteen year old, too. I'm glad they didn't tell that." The telephone rang and Chad got up and answered it. He held the receiver out to Sandy. "Hey, lover boy, it's your girlfriend."

Sandy shot Chad an evil look, went over, and took the receiver from him.

"Hello."

"Sandy, it's Gracie. I just saw you on television. Sandy, I was worried sick about you, and I missed you. I even got Momma to let me stay home today 'cause I couldn't stand to go to school worrying about you. Oh, Sandy, are you okay?"

Sandy was overcome with the strange feelings again. They weren't bad feelings, just strange ones that came upon him when he heard Gracie's voice and her caring words. Because of his lack of experience with girls, and all of this was totally new to him. He was glad his mother had gone back to the kitchen and his father's attention was riveted on Tim Deegan's forecast of the weather.

Chad, on the other hand, was making mooning faces at Sandy and pretending like he was giving a big kiss. Sandy turned his back to Chad and kept talking to Gracie.

"Yeah, Gracie, it was pretty heavy, but I'm okay. I missed you too. The ordeal was pretty horrible, but it's over now. I'll tell ya' all about it later. I did some stupid things that almost cost me my life.

"Sandy, I don't think you're stupid. You're only human, and humans make mistakes. You're okay. That's all that matters to me. I don't care about your boat. I mean I care that you lost it, but we'll have other times we can do things together. I can't wait to see you. Are you going to school tomorrow?"

"I don't think so. What I've been through in the past four days and three nights has pretty much worn me out. If my parents will let me, and I know they will, I'm gonna' sleep in and take it easy tomorrow. Gracie, I can barely stand up right now. If I hadn't loaded my boat with water, it would be even worse. You have no idea how scary the sharks were. I thought they were going to eat me."

"Oh, you poor thing. Sandy, don't take this wrong, but I want you to know that I really *like* you. You don't mind me saying that, do you?"

"Gosh, Gracie, nobody has ever said that to me before. No, I won't take it wrong." Sandy's feelings were on a circus ride, and he was struggling to make sense of them. But, he liked what he was experiencing. "Gracie, I never thought I'd say this to a girl, but I *like* you a lot, too. You're the first girl I've ever talked much to."

"Sandy, you are more of a man than any guy at Mayport Middle and certainly more decent. Sandy, I like you a lot, and it's because you are who you are. If Momma will let me skip school tomorrow, do you think we could get together?"

"Wow, Gracie, yeah! What would you say if I showed you around Mayport? We could eat lunch on the dock at Safe Harbor Seafood. See if she says okay and call me after ten in the morning. Gracie, I would like that a lot. I don't have a boat any more so I can't take you out and show you around like I promised."

"That's okay, Sandy. There will always be another time. I'm sure my Momma will say okay. I'll call ya' back later."

The kids said goodbye and hung up. Chad continued to tease Sandy until he went to bed. Sandy slept like he was dead that night. He hadn't even eaten supper, and Jeanette understood and didn't wake him.

CHAPTER X – EPILOGUE

Sandy and Gracie would become best of friends. Their relationship was one of innocence and respect. Sandy would gradually introduce Gracie to his world of nature and life. Gracie would introduce him to the world of girls and culture.

Sandy found himself in a youngster's dreamland. He had a best friend who was a girl and with whom he loved to spend time, because she never complained and always respected him and supported him. He had great parents. He had become a hero after all the news coverage on television and boldness against the bullies. Sandy could have done without the hero status. It was too much of a bother. And he was able to choose a boat that no other boy of fourteen had.

That's where it really got neat for Sandy. Steve knew boats and he knew the waters. He had insured *Out Back* for enough money to replace it with a brand new one. Sandy got a brand new fiberglass twenty-foot Carolina Skiff flats boat with a flat bottom, square prow, and a 150 hp Evinrude engine that he named *Don't Be Stupid.*